Winter

Angel

For the best part of me,

my daughter

Michaela Margaret

PART 1

As I look out the tiny window the snow is softly drifting. My memories drift to a year ago when my husband died. When our world changed. It's been very difficult this past year especially for my daughter. Nicole not having her father has made an emotional impact in her life as well as mine, but most of my concerns have been for her mental well-being in adjusting to this new chapter in life.

Bang! I hear what sounds like a suitcase hitting the floor. Come on Nicole, I exhale and loudly tell her the snow is starting to fall even faster. We're going to be late for this once in a lifetime adventure. She had come home from college just a few hours ago and should have already packed. Impatience now, I quip, come on hurry up and get those suitcases down here the taxi is going to be here any minute to pick us up for the airport.

I hear muffled mumbling and I know Nicole is saying something to me, and I probably don't want to know what it is.

The fluffy snowflakes begin to swirl faster as the wind begins to whip them around in swirls. It is getting colder fast. The snow falling was mesmerizing. This was the first winter snow of the season.

In a week, it will be a year since the event that changed our lives. It was an ordinary December Saturday with smells of cookie baking and twinkling Christmas lights. Richard and Nicole were wrestling on the living room floor. Bella, our giant poodle was barking and jumping over top of them. The sounds of laughter and barking suddenly stopped. I froze. Something was either broken or someone hurt. I dropped the cookie pan on the stove and rushed into the living room. Nicole was frantically shaking her dad to wake up. Bella sniffing his head, then licking his cheek. I knelt beside him and checked for a pulse. I looked at my daughter and told her to call 911 right now. I then began to give my husband CPR. I tried to calm myself by counting. Nicole's shaky voice said, I need help my dad is lying on the floor and has had a heart attack. Come quick. I tried not to look at her while I continued CPR, but from the corner of my eye, I could see she was terrified. I heard her rattled off the address and ask how long. It was less than four minutes that a bang rattled the front door. Reliving the moment in my mind I feel a shiver run through me.

Aloud clunk -bang startled me back to the present. Nicole began coming down the stairs with not a suitcase, but a very large suitcase. As she descends the stairs the suitcase is leaving black smudges on the walls as it swings in her hand. Do you need some help, honey? No, I got it, it's way too heavy for you mom.

Look, it's snowing, we're here and it's snowing and when we get to the Netherlands it's supposed to be snowing.

Nicole, did you know that no two... YEA, mom I know two snowflakes are alike. You seem to finish my sentences more and more. MOM, it's because you tell me the same things over and over. Wow, the snow is falling fast, will the trip be canceled? I am not sure, Nicole, it's in two hours, but planes fly in snow, I said. Nicole opened the front door letting snow dance into the foyer.

Uwe look at all the snow, Nicole squealed, I am going to make a snow angel for dad. Before I say anything to her about getting snow all over her, she plops down. I laugh seeing the big smirk on her little sweet angel face. Nicole lays down and yelps. Ouch, I hit my head on a rock she squints her eyes in pain and rubs her head. She lays back down gently and swings her arms up and down to make wings.

The taxi pulls up honking it's horn before it even stops. We looked at each other and smile. Here we go baby girl, a new adventure. The taxi driver, an older man with a crown of white hair and a beard to match tosses our carefully packed suitcases into a moldy smelly trunk. Nicole looks at the trunk then at me ready to say something. Well, it's not like the airline will be any more careful, I say, giving her a look that says, **don't say it**!

The driver says, so you are going on an adventure. "Yes, we are." The driver gently tugs on his beard thoughtfully and says, Life is an adventure.

We both get into the taxi, which to our surprise is clean and smells like roses. The taxi driver turns around and grins showing his bright white teeth and says, ok girls we'll get you to the airport in 10 minutes. As he turns around the taxi is already leaping forward.

The snow continues to fall faster even though the driver doesn't seem to notice the roads are covered in snow. I take Nicole's hand and squeeze it. She looks over to me and smiles. Mom, thanks for this trip, I know you did this for me, so Christmas wouldn't be so hard. Tears rim her eyes as she squeezes my hand. We both needed this trip, I said, wiping a tear that reached my cheek. She rested her head on my shoulder. I love you baby girl you are the best part of me and your dad. I hoped this trip would help us both heal from the loss and the many changes in our lives.

Nicole was having a difficult time trying to adjust to one parent who tried to play two parts. Her dad was her hero. She had lost her strong foundation. Her return to college was almost bewildering to her. I knew she would find her way. I didn't know it would take so long. I haven't had time to think about how my own life has changed or how I felt. I have put all my energy into helping her adjust. Late night trips to college to spend the night with her, then leaving by 5:00 am to make it home in time for me to get school were common. She was my whole life now.

Pulling curtly up to the curb, our driver had his door open before releasing his safety belt. Here we are girls, his said in a jolly tone. We emptied out and went to the back to retrieve our suitcase that were waiting for us. I paid and thanked him. He winked and said, Have a safe trip!

The snow was beginning to concern me as it continued to fall with larger wet snowflakes. Nicole was already through the doors turning to call to me to hurry up, we'll be late for the once in a lifetime adventure, mom!

The airport was bustling with all kinds of people who were trying to get to their plane. Pushing politely through the crowd we found our check in and dropped off our suit cases but kept our backpacks. We had already done an early check in, so all we had to do now is find our gate to go on.

"Mom, I am really thirsty, let's get something to drink before we go on", Nicole said walking further away from me into the crowds. Ok, ok, I say turning sideways this way and that way trying to catch up to her. Stopping in front of a juice bar we both ordered a Sunrise, which was quite refreshing. Now, I said, let's go find the gate we need. As she turned looking for the gate, I noticed she still had a few snowflakes stuck to the hood of her jacket. Before I could brush them away, she was off, with me trying to keep up with her in the crowds.

Finding our gate, we went in to stand in line, waiting entry. As we are waiting, I see Nicole watching a group of kids about her age laughing loudly. Are you looking at the boys or just listening, I ask her? Really mom, well listening, because I already have a boyfriend at college who cares about me. I already texted him to let him know we are ready to get on the plane. So, when do I get to meet Sam I ask curiously? It would have been Christmas, but since we are going away, maybe spring break. Ok, that sounds good I say.

I began to think how glad I was that she found a friend at school at a time she really needed one to help her get through. Being so young and losing a parent must devast your outlook on life, I couldn't imagine being her.

Finally, the call for our flight, then like cattle being herded to slaughter, we moved along a sweaty smelling narrow corridor into the plane. Of course, we were in the very back and had to squeeze past everyone else. I liked the back of the plane, it's the safest part, close to the bathrooms, and the kitchenette. Nicole was not so sure about my choices, since all the young people were in the middle of the plane. She hoisted her backpack into the overhead compartment along with mine. After settling in, Nicole announced that she was tired and was going to sleep. Ok, I thought, maybe I can watch a movie. I get out my glasses, then painstakingly get the movie menu up. Yep, it's *A Wonderful Life*, good movie this time of year.

I look over at my daughter's sweet sleeping face. Sleeping kids are angels. Being a 5th grade math teacher I truly believe that. There are days I want to say, "Ok class we are going to take a 30-minute nap". Nicole snores quietly, thank goodness. Her beautiful long light brown-red hair covering half of her face. Her face is so relaxed, and a little smirk is on her lips. I wonder what she is dreaming about.

Her stages of grief over the past year have been very difficult on her emotional and physical well-being. She was daddy's little girl and losing him was very traumatic for her. I often think she rather it be me who died instead her dad and somehow resents me being alive.

We had so much fun as family. We would go places together as a family. I realized, that the two of them shared a strong bond. I was the picture taker and was always on the side lines watching them. They were living life and I was watching it through a lens.

As the stewardess with her drink cart came by, I asked for a couple of waters. A young girl heading to the bathroom had to inch into our isle to get by. She said, so sorry I have to go. I smiled and said you gotta go you gotta go. I put the waters in our back-seat netting. I then did a selfie and posted it on Facebook with the headline "Once in a Life Time Adventure". I put my phone back into my belly-bag. I noticed Nicole was loosely holding her phone while she slept. I gently removed her phone from her half -opened hand and put it into my belly bag. Nicole hates belly bags and I must keep it covered under my shirt. She won't walk anywhere with me if I have it on the outside of my shirt.

I look around the plane. Most of the people are sleeping with airline blankets around their shoulders. The young people are on their phone with the overhead light shining a narrow beam onto their heads. I decided it was time for me to sleep because I didn't know how much I would get during the trip.

In my sleepy state I thought I heard my phone beeping, as I began to become aware, I realized the plane was tilted and white oxygen masks were hanging from the overhead. Now I was in a panic as was everyone else. I turned to Nicole who was still sleeping. The captain's voice came over the speaker asking the stewardess and passengers to get into the crash position. That's when panormium broke out. The screams and crying were deafening. Nicole didn't wake, I took my seat belt and hers and reconnected mine to hers. I bent my body over hers and bent my legs over top of hers. I could feel the plane moving faster in a downward slope. I cradled Nicole in my arms whispering I love you; I love you.

When the plane hit the ground there was an eerie silence. I thought, ok we made it. Then the thunderous sound and the plane was tilting, and all went silent and black.

The Wings of Mercy Hospital was having a neurosurgeon convention when the call came in that Flight 121 had 77 dead and 44 survivors. All doctors were called to assist. At first, I heard beeping sounds far off. I then began to force myself awake, fearing the crash wasn't over. Then I heard a woman saying my name asking me to open my eyes. I tried moving but couldn't and forced my eyes to open. The lights were on and a young nurse was staring straight at me. You are in the hospital, the plane crashed. She took my hand and said your daughter is right here next to you. I turned my head slightly to see my baby girl, in a bed with tubes and air mask on her.

How is she? Will she make it? I could hear my voice rising. The nurse said, the doctor will be in to speak to you in a few moments. The nurse took Nicole's hand and put it into mine. As I clasped her hand it was warm. That's a good sign. I tried to turn my body to face her, but I just couldn't move. The nurse said, just rest I will be back with the doctor.

I could see the doorway. The nurse had a white coat in her hands. A tall man with white hair gave her his coat which looked brownish-red and put on the white coat the nurse held out to him. She handed him a chart and said the test results came back.

He turned and entered the room. Ms. Goodwin, I am Dr. Vinke. I want to talk to you about your injuries and your daughter's.

Ok, just give me the facts, no maybes or possible, just what is wrong with us I say in the firmest voice I can muster.

The doctor looks at our hands clasped together, and smiles. Well, first I will tell you about your daughter's condition. She is in a coma, she has no brain activity, the machines are keeping her alive.

You mean she will never wake up?

No, I am sorry, she will never wake up. We are keeping her alive so that you could have time to say good bye and if you would donate her heart. I know this is a lot to take in and I have just told you some very distressing news, but time is of the essence.

The doctor then put his hand on top of ours. Your injuries, Mrs. Goodwin, are very grave. Your seatbelt severed your body in half. We don't have enough organs to replace the ones you have damaged. I looked down at the bed…… The bottom half of the bed was flat. No, no, no, I didn't want to think about it. What are you saying?

With tears in his eyes, the doctor looked at me. I am saying that you have about an hour or two to be with your daughter.

Wait, you are saying that we both going to die? I have no body and she is brain dead. And… you want me to sign an organ donor form?

Yes, I am so sorry. Do you have anyone we can contact for you? Would you like a priest to come?

She is too young to die! Ok, wait a minute, can I donate my brain to my daughter? I don't have a complete body, but I have a brain. Can you put my brain in her body? She is too young she will…. I broke off not knowing how to finish that sentence.

The doctor looking stunned, managed to get his voice, and say, well it's – it's, possible. It's an emergency and both of you are donors and same blood type. After what seemed like hours, the doctor turned and said YES, I can do that.

He saw my puzzled look and guessed that I wondered how he could. You see, I am a neurosurgeon, I was here today for a conference. The operation would require a neurosurgeon to complete it.

Then, there must be a reason you are my doctor today. My hopes rising. So, we can do this?

Not sure of what I was really getting into. I always relied on my husband to slow me down. Was I making the right choice? We would both die today and yet part of us would live today, two becoming one.

The nurse came in with sad eyes and looked at the doctor. She said is there anything I can do? Dr. Vinke jerked up his head and said, get me two organ donor forms, Dr. Lambs, and operating room 3 stat!

The nurse looking flush, said right away doctor, and rushed off.

Well, Ms. Goodwin, I am going to the operating room, a few orderlies will be here to take both you and your daughter up.

As he got up from the bed, the nurse reentered the room with forms and a pen. Here are the forms you requested. Aww, good, here Ms. Goodwin, I need you to sign both forms, then he left.

Wow was I really going to do this. Yes, I am, I took the pen and signed the bottom of both papers, just as a few men came into the room. The nurse took the papers from me and said that I would be going to operating room 3.

When we reached the operating room, both of us were wheeled in side by side. Dr. Vinke took my hand and introduced me to the other doctor, Dr. Lambs. We are going to operate at the same time to make the transfer of your brain into your daughter's body. We will also, skin graph your finger skin or prints to you. This way you will be you in a manner of speaking. Other matters we will discuss later. The operation will take about 5 to 7 hours. You will wake up in few days. I will have you sedated to give your body time to heal. I will come and check on you each morning and evening. Are you ready?

Yes, I am I said in a strong voice. Alright, then, count back from 100, 99, 98, 9……

There is that beeping sound. I feel sleepy, yet I want to wake up, that beeping sound again, what is it?

My eyes are so heavy, I can barely open them. The beeping gets louder and faster. Someone touches my hand and says, "Hey sleepy head can you open your eyes for me?" I manage to open my eyes into slits and see an elderly nurse bending over me. Great, she says. Do you know your name?

My name is Lisa Goodwin. Great, she says again, and askes do you know what year it is? It's, um, 2024, right? She smiles, Yes, it is. What is today, I ask. It's Christmas Day, now, I am going to get Dr. Vinke to see you. He has been waiting for you to wake up. The nurse turns and leaves the room.

Within minutes both doctors hurriedly entered the room. Dr. Vinke reached out and took my wrist. Ms. Goodwin do you know where you are? The other doctor was busy taking note of the beeping machines.

Well, a hospital, I am not sure where, there was a ...... I am not sure.

It's ok, Ms. Goodwin, give it time you have been through a traumatic ordeal and your mind and body need time to heal and reason it mentally.

I looked at him with a questioning gaze. He seemed to understand and began to speak softly. You and your daughter were in a plane crash in the Netherlands. Both of you were brought here to The Wings of Mercy Hospital. Your daughter had hit her head and was brain dead. You were severed in half from your seatbelt. Your injuries were so severe that you had only hours to live. You wanted to donate your brain into your daughter's body. During surgery we also skin grafted your finger skin to her fingers. Your heart was donated to a young girl also from the plane crash.

Yes, I remember, the beeping sounds. Dr. Lambs looked over, then turned the sound off. I am ok right?

Well, Ms. Goodwin that is what we will see over the next few weeks. We have set you up for a psychiatrist starting today and physical therapy tomorrow. Your surgery was very successful. We removed your brain below the Pons and connected your brain into Nicole's body. Since both of you were related or had the same DNA and blood types all went well. Ms. Goodwin you were; shall we say, the original and your daughter the copy. It was very interesting that in your case since your brain was the older organ it took well in a younger body with minimal swelling.   So, we will be doing more research in that area. I will be checking on you each morning and evening as well as Dr. Lambs. After your psychiatrist gives the ok, someone from the airlines, the American embassy and police will also want to speak to you as well.   Before that even happens, we will discuss your surgery and what that means for you for the future.

Well now, that's a lot to take in. Is there any chance of getting some pepperoni pizza? I don't know why I am asking; I just have this overwhelming craving for pizza.

The doctors laughed. Dr. Vinke chuckled as he said you are getting better. No, pizza for a few days though you will be on soft foods like gelatin until all the medications have passed through your body. Dr. Lambs smiled and said in a soothing voice, you will be fine. They both left in deep conversation.

What now I thought. I look at my hands, arms and under the covers. Not my body. This is my baby girl's body. What now what now! Do I have to have a funeral, for who, me or Nicole? What will I tell family and friends? They will see Nicole not me. What about work? I was going to retire two years. Do I have to work another 30 years? What will I say when I get back to American, to home? Did I make the right choice? Yes, why should we both die. We are, well, still alive. I am not Nicole, I don't talk like her, or act like her. I do sound and look like her. So, will others see me as Nicole. Will they see my choice as selfish?

Just then, the door swished open and in came the kindest looking old lady. She was short in a soft blue suit with her gray hair up in a stylish do for her age. Her voice was sweet and made you want to just listen to her voice. Good afternoon, Ms. Goodwin, I am Dr. Greta Homestead, the psychiatrist. I will be meeting with you each day. Dr. Lambs has spoken with me about your loss and injuries and the special circumstances you are in.

Your surgery is not a typical one, she went on. You have donated your heart to another child, and donated your brain to another child, your daughter. How we feel about our heart is different than the way we feel about our brain. Although your surgery isn't the first of its kind it is the first time with a mother and daughter. We will work together to make you feel like you and what you want in life.

I was so calmed by her voice; I didn't even realize she had stopped talking and was staring at me. Oh, yes that sounds good, I, have, a lot of well, dumb questions, and I do mean a lot. I don't even know where to begin. Like, how weird is hearing my thoughts and my daughter's voice saying them.

Call me Greta, may I call you Lisa? Sure. Ok, Lisa, let's start with what is on your mind.

I know this sounds strange, but do you have a mirror, I ask. Greta finds one in the bathroom and brings it out and puts it face down on the table. When you are ready, she says. Now, tell me about Lisa.

Uhm, I know I am me in my daughter's body. I don't know how to put it. My daughter isn't with me, her body is, and voice is. I miss her cute smirky smile and quick wit. I miss her. How can I tell family and friends she is gone when all they see is her, not me? She is gone, the spirit of Nicole is gone. Then, the flood gate of tears came so violently I could not see nor speak.

Quite some time passed, before I could even speak. I am sorry; I am such a cry-baby; I say it tiny little girl's voice.   Greta got up and took all the tissues I had used and put them in the waste-paper basket. She slowly sat down and looked directly at me. Lisa, you have been through a very traumatic experience and tears help to heal and let you move on.   So, I said, I will probably be doing a lot of crying!

She gently took my hand, and said, Lisa you are alive in a different body. You have lost your daughter but not your mother's love or memories of her.   You gave your heart to another child to live. That family is very grateful to you. Your daughter loved you. If the roles had been reversed, what would your daughter have done.

I freeze for a moment, trying so hard to control myself. Then, I laugh so hard tears stream down my face. I can hardly breathe I was laughing so hard. My daughter would have looked at my body and said, EW, I got stuck with Pillsbury dough-boy's body. At that comment, Greta to; started laughing.

The laughter felt so good to my soul. I could just picture it and hear her voice saying it.   Greta wiped her tears of laughter away and said well, I am going to leave on that note, and will still be laughing all the way home. I will come tomorrow before your physical therapy.

Great, I will see you tomorrow, and I really meant it. She left, and somehow, I felt so terribly lonely and wanted her to come back and stay with me.

I picked up the mirror. No hair, but sutures encompassed behind one ear all round to the other ear. I thought of Frankenstein pieced together. I put a towel over my head and saw my beautiful baby girl. I love you so much and don't know how to do this. Since I have her voice, I reply, "**Ma, you got this, just make sure you make the most of it, and get a puppy.**" This is what she would have said to me.

An orderly came in a few minutes later with a tray of food. He was short and clean-cut young man. Here you go ma'am; I will be back in an hour for the tray. Oh wait, um, I don't think I can eat anything with wheat. Yes, ma'am it was listed on your chart CD we make everything gluten free and peanut free. Thank you. I had the Celiac gene and my symptoms were slight. However, Nicole had severe symptoms. One little crumb would make her sick, and ill feeling for days sometimes weeks. It took months for the body to heal itself. In Europe CD is common so finding food and restaurants is much easier than in America.

I lifted the lid hoping for something good. It's not an America hospital, maybe the food is better here. Yea right, not better. Two orange jello packs, with hot water, tea bag, two sugars, and scrambled eggs, maybe. Really, I felt pity, then stupid, just because I went through, an ordeal, doesn't mean I am going to get steak dinner, or pizza for that matter.

A few tears tumbled down my cheek while I ate, and I hurriedly swiped them away so no one could see. The hospital room I was in had a curtain pulled aside to expose the wall of glass windows and door. I could see all the way down the hallway. The room was painted a pale soft blue and clouds on the ceiling.

I found the TV remote and turned it on. Funny watching a TV show from America with subtitles. I watched and looked down the hallway from time to time. How long would I be here, I wondered?

The elderly nurse came back. Her name tag read Mary. Hi Mary, I said. Well, have you finished your dinner she asked kindly? Yes, I well, am still a little hungry. Well, I will get you a muffin, what kind would you like? Blueberry please, also, I must go to the bathroom, can I walk to it, I don't want to use a bed pan. Sure, dearie let me help you. Since this is the first time getting up, I will have to help you until you get back into bed. Alrighty then, I said. She held my arm and lead me out of bed into the bathroom. She helped me lift the gown so I could go. Really, I try not to show my surprise at the Brazilian wax job. What was Nicole thinking getting a wax job down there? It's soooo hard to pee when someone is standing there. Finally, finished she walked me back to bed. That's a pretty tattoo on your back. WHAT tattoo on my back? Show me. Mary walked me back to the bathroom and used the mirror on the back of the door for me to see into the mirror above the sink. I pulled up the gown and above my butt, and there was a giant flowering scroll in reds, purples, greens, and blues. Oh my gosh, I have a tramp-stamp! Mary laughed, and soon I was too. It is rather pretty isn't it? She walked me back to bed and tucked me in still chuckling. I will get you that blueberry muffin. I smiled and thanked her.

I laid back into bed hoping to get sleep, but questions just swirled in my mind. My daughter's mind and spirit were gone. Just the shell of her body remained. I am me, in Nicole's body. My head started to ache. I couldn't think about all this right now. One day a time, and one problem at a time I told myself.

I must have been tired because when I woke a lunch tray was on my bedside table. Well, let's see if lunch is better than dinner. No, it's not as I put the plate cover back on top of the jello and mystery broth. I noticed a cloth napkin with something in it. I unwrapped it to find the blueberry muffin. Yes, Mary came through. I happily wolfed down the muffin.

I lay my head back and just closed my eyes when the door opens, and Greta pushing a wheelchair greets me warmly. How, I wish I had that kind of calming effect. Good afternoon Lisa, how are you feeling today? I am, that's a loaded question you must ask all your patients, right? She laughed and said, "I never thought of that." I brought you a head scarf to keep your head warm. Let me know if you'd rather a cap or hat. I like scarves it's pretty too. Greta expertly wraps it around my head.

Lisa, if you like I can wheel you to the flower room downstairs. Umm, sounds good to me cause the smell of the mystery broth is making me nauseas. As Greta helped me into the wheel chair she started telling me about the young girl who got my heart. Her name was Angela and she was with her grandparents on the flight. The grandparents survived and are currently staying with their granddaughter on another floor of the hospital. Since you donated your heart, there is question I would like to pose to you. Would you like to meet the young lady?

Wow, this is getting deep I thought. You know Greta, I would like to meet her. It seems to me it's kind a weird cause now that I think about it, if she has my heart, how is the donor; me; still walking around.

Ahh, very good Lisa, you are very smart, but then I read your file and it said you were a math teacher. Yes, I am, and of course math teachers are the smartest, I say smiling. Well, part of your recovery is how you see and feel about yourself and in your case who you are, Greta said in firm tone.

I had to think about that last part and remained silent until we reached the flower room. Flowers from floor to ceiling filled the room with the pleasant aroma of Lilies. I love this room, and as someone who loves flowers felt relaxed and almost at home.

So, Lisa what do you think about yourself and how do you feel about meeting the girl, she asks. Greta, your questions are heavy duty I say! Well, I am me in Nicole's body. Stop for a moment, Greta said in a whisper, think about yourself as body and mind, you can't be both. I never thought about this stuff in depth, only once with a friend while eating Haagen-Dazs chocolate-chocolate chip.

Geeze, ok, well people have mind or brain and a soul. So, I am thinking, people who get a different heart or an artificial heart aren't different people and they would still have a soul. Sometimes we say heart and soul, or I like essences or Arora about us which I don't know if it's the brain. For instance, someone who has what I would call a good heart or soul, who would; say; run into a burning house to rescue people without thinking; have a good soul or essences. Our brain is our soul making us do good or bad I say thoughtfully.

I look at Greta and realize what she is trying to get me to see. I am Lisa, with a tramp-stamp, tighter butt, and stand up boobs. Greta's eyes get wide and she begins laughing so hard I can see she is trying to catch her breath, which makes me start laughing till my belly hurts.

You got me on that one Lisa, I did not see that coming Greta replies. RIGHT, I say.

This makes sense now; I was trying to figure out when I get home who I should have a memorial for. It should be for Nicole; her soul is in heaven. She left me the gift of her body that I needed.

Greta walks around the wheel chair and starts pushing me back to the room. I must get you back because your physical therapy will be in 10 minutes, Greta says. As we enter my room a big, and I mean big black dude in a white uniform is waiting for us. Whoa, I say, not the rubber room. The man looks at me quizzically then smiles. No ma'am I am your physical therapist. As they do the hand off, I am wheeled into the elevator with silence. So, what's your name I asked. Bud. Ok Bud, you're not going to hurt me, are you? Maybe; we'll see. Umm, I start thinking to myself, maybe we didn't get off on the right foot. I wonder if they have nurse's call button in the therapy room.

It's a room, I thought it would be like a gym size, but it was a decent size room. As Bud sits and double checks my chart, he says Ma'am this will be our plan of action today, walking, step ups, leg lifts, arm lifts. Hey that sounds easy peeze I say. After almost an hour I am in a sweat. I didn't realize simple things would be so, so, sweaty. Bud smiles and says you have been in bed for about 3 days so tomorrow should be easier. So, can I walk back to my room? Bud had me pushing the wheelchair back to the room as a compromise. See you tomorrow Bud.

Back in my hospital bed, I soon become restless. I don't want to think too much; I figure I must give my brain a rest. I decide to walk around and get to know my surroundings since I don't know how long I will be here. Being the curious sort, I would like to think, not nosey I look into each room as I walk by. Some people are trying to sound cheery, some just crying quietly, others just sitting staring out the windows. At the end of the hall is a waiting room with a young man holding a fussy baby and an elderly man with him trying to calm the baby. I can tell he is holding the baby wrong, so he must be a first- time dad. I walk over and say, may I? He carefully hands me the baby and I hoist the baby across my chest and begin to rock gently, the fussiness stops, and the baby begins to close his sleepy eyes. Both men afraid to speak in fear of waking the baby watch. Babies like to hear your heart beat it calms them. I lift the sleeping baby and put him into his father's arms the right way. Both men smile and mouth THANK YOU as I leave. I realize then that the heart beat is Nicole's.

When I got back to my room, I saw a napkin bundle on my table. I opened it to find a warm blueberry muffin, thank you God for Mary. Today's special is lime jello and still a mystery broth. I pushed the nurse's button. Mary came rather quickly. Thank you, Mary, I now know that God loves me to have sent you to be my nurse. She chuckles and asks if I need anything. I want to take a shower and get a fresh johnnie gown in pink maybe? I will see what I can find for you dearie. I want to take her home she would make a great mom. After about 15 minutes Mary came back with pink gown. She said, I went to the children's ward as they have both colors, grown-ups only get blue. I am not a grown-up today; you are the BEST Mary.

After my shower I went to sit by the window overlooking the front lawn of the hospital. I thought about all that had happened that day. I started to feel self-conscious about what I said and thought. Meet the girl who has my heart, the heart I used for the past 44 years, that gave birth to Nicole. Holding the baby to Nicole's heart to soothe him, getting a child's pink gown. Maybe this isn't as simple as I thought it would be. My heart ached and the tears kept me company through the night.

When Greta and I were sitting in the flower room the next day I told her about the day before. It seems like when I get this fixed in my head, then all sudden all these thoughts start tearing apart what I think I know. Greta takes my hand and says; Lisa, what has happened to you is quite tragic and amazing and trying to fix it in your head might take long time, and not be what you should focus on right now. Let's focus on the present, your grief, your gift to another girl, who you are now.

I miss my daughter. This morning when I went to the bath room I looked in the mirror and saw her, my beautiful baby girl. She looked back at me and said, **quit your whining**. That's what she would have said. I feel her essence somehow within me. It's not a bad thing, it's comforting. To know that another person is alive because of me is well, cool. As to who I am, well me, I don't look like me, I can also say I don't feel like me, because I have way more energy now than I did a week ago. I feel like jogging, which is what Nicole used to do. Greta smiled and said you are off to a good start.

After Bud, the Punisher I like to call him, said I was fit as a fiddle. I could picture him playing a fiddle at a country store. I sat in the chair looking out the window when the doctors both came in with a box, and it looked like a box that I would kill for. Ms. Goodwin, Dr. Lambs said grinning ear to ear, we brought you something special. Is it pepperoni? Yes, I believe so. Oh, was it great! The doctors had some as well, joking that I shouldn't tell anyone about this nutritional faux pas as they had a reputation. Dr. Lambs laughed and said, I hear you are doing well with your physical therapy. Oh well, yea I feel like running a marathon like really running, my daughter used to run every day. If you feel up to it there is a jogging path in the back of the hospital near the garden. Sure, but these bootie socks wouldn't last every long. Dr. Vinke wiped his mouth and walked over to the closet and opened it. There to my surprise there were our back packs and my belly bag. Ok, then no excuses, I will be jogging. We laughed, Dr. Vinke said that sounds like a commercial.

Dr. Vinke sat down and said, Ms. Goodwin I would like to talk to you about your health. I felt like the ball was going to drop. I sat down on the bed and looked at him. Ok, what's the bad news. No, no bad news, it's the opposite, you are doing great and Dr. Homestead says that you are doing so much more than most you will be able to leave here much sooner than expected. What I want to talk about is how you view yourself. The surgery we did is not legal in America and you are an American. It is a very important medical advancement. In your case, you and your daughter are not the first parent and child to undergo donorship surgery, nor the first case of brain donorship. You are however, the first shall we say an American in a foreign country to donate your child's organs to combine the organs with one of yours's.

Whoa, I didn't think of that problem. Like you're saying the press or radical groups who would oppose this type of donorship. Wouldn't my daughter's and my medical records private? I don't want people judging me, sending me hate mail, or gawking at me. I feel as though I am me and my daughter is gone and left me the gift of her organs so that I could live. I would have gladly given all of me for her to live instead of me. I even have my own finger prints.

The doctors looked at each other then back at me. Dr. Vinke said in a quiet tone, yes you are right. Your records are private. We have your daughter's and yours labeled X & Y even Dr. Homestead has your label as Y. This way your privacy is secured. Three things I want you to know. First, our hospital administrator and the American Embassy consul general we will meet you before the gendarmerie and airline insurance investigators. Second, who you are and what that means for your future we will discuss with Dr. Homestead and you. Third, because your case is unique, we would like to continue monitoring your health over the next 10 years for our research with doctors in America.

This will cost another pepperoni pizza. The doctors stared at each other, then Dr. Vinke said ok, with onions to get some veggies in there. We all laughed feeling the relief from the intense moments. They left the room looking over my chart. Wait, I yelled, they both turned and looked at me. Hey docs, can I get my file to YU instead of Y. They looked at me thoughtfully and Dr. Lambs said; sure, I like it.

I looked at the still open closet door with the backpacks inside. We had packed them for two days,

• • •

just in case the airline lost our luggage. I felt weird going through my daughter's belongings. I open the back pack and start to weep. Inside carefully wrapped was this year's Christmas ornament. Every year since she was born; we made an ornament. This was a snowflake with a picture of her dad and her smiling. Carefully rewrapping the ornament, I put it back in the pack. I get up and go to the bathroom to splash some cold water on my face. When I look into the mirror, I see the most beautiful girl who I love so much it hurts. I try to smirk like she did, I love that little smirk she would give me. Maybe wider, and less teeth showing. I give up and go back to the back pack. I pull out her jogging suit, socks, sneakers, bra, and **oh H to the NO** I am not wearing butt floss. I open the other back pack and find a real pair of underwear.

It is stinking cold out here, did she really plan on running. I start jogging to get warm and begin what turned out to be an hour run. I felt tired but I felt great like I wanted to do it again later on. I would do this every day, just like Nicole did. I really enjoy it. I went back to my room and showered and changed into my pjs, they were loosely comfortable. I got my fanny pack and pulled out our phones. I turn on my phone to see the date was December 27th. It's been 6 days since we left America. Did anyone know, certainly the news would have reported how many American passengers, and even if they didn't know our flight number, we haven't called or Facebooked anything. Maybe I should talk to Greta before I call or send any IMs or Facebook. I plug in both phones to charge. I check my e-mails, so much junk and soon the phone slips onto the bed as I turn over to sleep.

I again wake up around lunch time. There is another napkin, and yes Mary comes through again. Folks, today's lunch special is a bologna sandwich with yellow jello. By the time I finish, Greta comes through the door. I jump up still in my jammies. I toss on the pink hospital gown and say ok let's go the flower room. As we walk, I explain to her that I don't know what to say to family, friends, work! She explained that after a plane crash, and on-line board and phone numbers are set up so people can check on loved ones. Therefore, most likely someone knows. People calling the hospital are told that patients will be able to contact them as soon as possible and they may leave phone messages. Have you checked the messages on the phone by your bed? No, I didn't have my glasses. How dumb am I, I don't need glasses anymore to read! This is going to take time to get used to. Yes, it will. We can discuss what you want to share with others and talk about what makes you feel comfortable.

Well, first of all I don't want anyone to know that I am in her body, although they would see and hear Nicole. I can't pretend I am Nicole, well, actually I could, but I want to be me, a teacher, ready to retire in a couple of years, not go to graduation this spring at Rowan and start a job for the next 30 years.

Greta takes both my hands and says well, from your passport photo you two looked a lot alike. You had red hair short, and your daughter's is well, long and light reddish brown. Maybe if you styled and colored your hair you would look more like your old self.

My old self, eh, I caught that. She smiled and said, people seeing others after a tragedy don't always look at the details as grief and pain overshadow them.

So, if I dye my hair then cut it into the style I usually have and buy new smaller "old lady" clothes I should look more like me. But my skin is so young. We have the same eyes, nose, cheeks, and mouth. I could wear fake glasses. Yea, the skin thing is bothering me. Wait, maybe I could say my skin was so damaged they had to regenerate it. Does that sound too SCI-FI?

Ok, Greta, one day at a time. I can do this. I can say that Nicole didn't make it and that I was critically injured in the crash. The doctors had to put me back together and I don't quite look the same. I would like to do a memorial service for Nicole when I get home. I feel; her friends and I need closure.

Greta grinned. It sounds like you have a plan of how to cope with the new life situation.

As we walked down the hall for my physical therapy, Greta took my hand and said, you have a strong resilience that will help you each and every day. Some days Greta, I need you to help me make sense of it all.

Bud was ready with some small weights. Ok today we start strength training. I was surprised how well I did, and so was Bud adding more and more. I knew I couldn't have done that amount of weight, but Nicole being 23 years younger than me; could. I died I tell myself, by body was cut in half, I needed a whole body for my brain to live. My body died but Nicole's is walking around. Bud seeing my distraction said, focus on one thing at a time only. Yea, I say, that will be my motto for today. One thing at a time.

After therapy I went for another run which I pushed myself to the limit. Wow, this body was fast and had endurance. In my old body, maybe I would jog one tenth of a mile if that.

I decided it was time to listen to the messages on the phone. After a few failed attempts I finally got the hang of it. My sister and brothers called along with my girlfriend Margaret. I smiled with tears streaming down my face. How would I tell them that Nicole wasn't coming home? When Richard had died a year ago, people treated me differently. Now, I am husband and childless. Would people look at me with pity? Going back to work would be hard facing people and their uncomfortableness.

After a few more days, I was ready to email family and friends. With counseling from Greta and Dr. Vinke I was going to let them know about Nicole. I called my sister then brothers, since both my parents were gone. Then, I emailed friends and friends from work. I emailed my principal and also explained that I would not be back to work as I am still in the hospital in the Netherlands and did not know when I would be able to fly. My head is shaved so I don't need to worry about the color, and I put on the head scarf. Nicole never wore make -up but I always have. So, I put on some make up and put my glasses on and did a selfie in the hospital bed. I kept the overhead lights on low. Then, I put the picture up on Facebook with a quick explanation of the crash. Here we go; I thought. I decided I wouldn't read any messages for at least another day and give myself a breather. So grateful to who ever invented Copy and Paste.

On New Year's Eve, Greta came on time as usual. This time however, her smile didn't reach her eyes. I began to look worried and she picked up on it. Lisa, we are going to meet with Dr. Vinke and the American Embassy consul general. I will be there as well. I looked at Greta and said, there is no bad news is there? No, none that I know of. No stressor, Lisa, remember your motto focus one day at a time.

When we enter the small office of Dr. Vinke we all sat almost touching as the office was so small. Dr. Vinke asked me how I was doing today. Fine. Good, we are waiting for Mr. Dupree from the embassy he should be here any moment. Ms. Goodwin your labs results are all in normal range. It means you will be able to leave soon. The airline is handling all the costs of your care and future yearly visits to a neurosurgeon. Your own personal insurance company will not be privy to your medical records since the airline litigators have taken care of all medical costs.

Dr. Lambs has found a neurologist near your home in America, who is also in a research facility. He has all the contact information for you. We will give you your file with the information of your surgery. Your name is not on it, it reads YU. I chuckle then stop by the stern look on Dr. Vinke's face. We discussed with the doctor the sensitive nature of your surgery. You will only give the file to Dr. Light only, not any nurses. This way it should keep your records secure. Right, I say, I feel like a spy with my most secret documents. At that moment, an impeccably dressed, short balding man with a handle bar mustache entered the room.

His presence commanded respect and we all stood. He introduced himself with a slight accent. We all shook hands and sat. Mr. Dupree turned to me and took my hand. I am so sorry for your loss. I am at your service madame. Thank you for your kindness, I say. Dr. Vinke has explained the sensitive nature of your organ donation and this situation bears special handling. He tells me that you do not wish for anyone to know of your organ donation of your daughter's body. The news of an American doing this type of say organ donation in a foreign country would not be good news reading. I want to be absolutely certain that you understand the complications that could arise should this information get into the news media. That is correct, I don't want anyone to know, I say in a shaky voice.

Mr. Dupree looks at Dr. Vinke and says, how is the hospital handling Ms. Goodwin and her daughter's medical records?

Dr. Vinke said; Ms. Goodwin has her own finger prints, and we are treating it as her daughter did not survive.

This seems clear cut then. Ms. Goodwin, we will issue you a new passport and driver's license. We will take a picture of you now. Also, there is the matter of the airline investigators. Ms. Goodwin they will contact you about getting permission for medical records, such as the death certificate for your daughter and records of your treatment. They are very discreet as they too do not wish for any news media to get wind of a daughter-mother sacrifice. I can tell you that they are offering $100,000 for the death of a family member and another $50,000 for those injured plus their medical costs. Now, if you wish to sue for other damages, wrongful death then it would take years. We can discuss this later, before you meet with them and the police. I will be with you. Think of any questions you want to know. I will contact you in two days and we will discuss anything you think of before meeting with them.

While we are here, I do have one question, the remains? Could I get them cremated before I go, so I can take them with me? I wanted to have a memorial for my daughter when I get home. Also, I kinda understand the new passport and driver's license, but why?

Mr. Dupree said in a soft fatherly tone. We want your ids to be as close to your current appearance as possible, so no questions are asked. I will take care of all that for you. He got out his phone and said, don't smile just look into the lens. After he took my picture, he again took my hand and said, I will speak to you again in two days, you are a very brave woman. If you need anything this is my card you may contact me at any time.

Greta got up and told Mr. Dupree she would see him out. They left. I looked at Dr. Vinke and said, I have a question. Sure, he said. I have a lot of energy and want to run. My daughter ran but I never have. Oh, he smiled. Her body was used to running and some of the hormones your brain will get a que from.

Just like the Celiac, so I have basically all her body specific conditions. Aww, does that mean I will have a period? I just went through menopause and was over it, won't my brain tell the body, that I am older and over that.

I am sorry for smiling at your discomfort, Dr. Vinke covers his mouth. Your brain is reading the hormones in your body and the body says you are young and sorry you will have your period. Was your daughter on birth control?

This is not funnnny or right. I don't want to go through another 20 years of periods; really! Dr. Vinke turned away in his chair. I see you laughing and snickering. May your wife have triplets. Ha, that made you stop laughing. He turned back to face me with his eyes smiling. I am really sorry for laughing, but it's the way you say it makes it funny. I start laughing too.

I leave his office for my physical therapy session. Hey Bud, what kind of pain do you have for me today?

We are going to start you on the treadmill and see if you can do two miles. It should take about 25 minutes. Bah, I can do that in 5 minutes. Hey, I will bet you a gluten-free pepperoni pizza I can? Bud not one to miss a challenge, says you're on. Time starts now. What, I jump onto the treadmill and begin to pick up my pace. I start laughing to myself, since I haven't told him I have been running the last few days.

Ok, so, tomorrow I will bring soda Bud; because pizza tastes better with soda! See ya!

As I walk back to my room, I decide to take the elevator to the baby wing. Standing in front of a window watching little bundles of joy sleeping is so peaceful. I wrap my arms around myself, I miss you baby girl. As I look at my reflection in the window, I imagine her, what would she say. She would say, **Mom, stop being a creeper and get back to your own room.** I laugh. She would say that. I can really hear it.

I get back to my room to find todays special- a salad, mixed veggies, lime jello, an omelet and juice. I wonder if this might be the real reason people in here don't smile. There was no blueberry muffin as Mary had the day off. She would be back on duty tomorrow, I couldn't wait. I realize, tomorrow is the New Year and I am on a once in a life time adventure. I decide to change and jog around the garden path. It was getting late and starting to get dark, but I needed air. I wonder if Nicole ran when she needed time to think?

By the time I walk back inside it's dark out. I push the button to the elevator it slides open and a young man is inside. He smiles and I get into the elevator. I push my floor and see he is one above me. The elevator music is the same I think all over the world. The young man says, do you work here? No, I am patient. I don't usually dress like this but, I jogged around the garden. Well, he said, you look to be in pretty good shape; my name is Thijs my sister is a nurse here. Now, that is a cool name, I would have no idea how to spell it but it's a cool name. Oh, my name is Lisa. I felt like saying and old enough to be your mother but bit my tongue to stop laughing. As the door slide opened, I turned and said, nice to meet you, Thijs with the cool name. Smiling wide, he said, see you Lisa with the jogging clothes.

I went to bed to wake up at lunch time again. Today's special is something swimming around in red sauce, yellow jello, and a roll. The best part, a napkin with a blueberry muffin, yea Mary is back.

Today is the first day of the new year. I am debating over picking up my phone to read e-mails and check the status on Facebook. Do I want to start the new year with sorrow? No, I don't. Just thinking of my baby girl makes it hard to breathe. I went into the bathroom and looked in the mirror. Hey baby girl, Happy New Year! I imagine what she would say, and since it's her voice it has a warm calming effect. She says, **Mom, you can do this, stop wearing those granny panties, and make sure you dress me cool and not like an old lady always wearing flowers, and it's time to get a puppy for Bella.** Are these the things I really think she would say or is she saying them literally?

Nicole always wanted a Czechoslovakian Wolf dog. Maybe I should look into it while I am here. I get back into bed to contemplate this decision. Just then, Greta comes in. Hey Greta, I didn't think I would see you until tomorrow. I know, she says, but today is the first day of the New Year and I thought you could use some company. I tell her about my episode in the bathroom mirror. She laughs and says, sounds like you knew your daughter pretty well.

It doesn't escape me that she said "knew" as in past tense. I have to get used to that and not let it bother me. I smile at her and say; do you think it's strange for me to talk to her in the mirror?

No, not at all; everyone deals with tragic events in various ways. Your tragic event is certainly one that hasn't been studied of course, but I think that since you find it calming it is a good thing that will help you adjust to your new situation. You will be looking in the mirror every day, make it positive. Ok then, Greta tell me about this country what are your favorite places to see and the best foodie places? We talked for over an hour before she left.

I get some change from my belly bag and go to the vending machine and choose two grape Fanta sodas and skip to physical therapy. Bud did not disappoint and no pain today just chewing exercises.

I decided to change and do a jog before dinner and was feeling pretty good about the day. I felt sad, but not the overwhelming sad today.

Once I finished the jog I came back inside and stared out the window at the garden area. It would be lovely come spring. Hi, Lisa with the jogging clothes. I turn around to see Thijs. Hello Thijs with the cool name. He came over and said Happy New Year, and here is some Erwtensoep he took from the wicker basket he was holding. It was a very hot mason jar with some green soup I guessed. Wow, thanks, what is it? We eat this thick pea and rook worst sausage soup in winter. I was bringing a few jars up for my sister. Thank you, I say, this looks way better than the dinner here. It is very kind of you, I hope you have a wonderful New Year! He smiled and said, I am running late, but I hope to see you again and off he went. Well, I thought I have to remember he sees Nicole; not me an old lady, or middle- aged woman.

Back in my room I showered and got into my pink gown and decided to eat the soup. Let me tell you this was the best pea soup I ever had. It was very thick, and the sausage was just delectable. I could eat this every day; it was right on the top of the list with the blueberry muffin.

What other kinds of great food do they have here? I get on my phone and decide to email Mr. Dupree about the historical and food places in town. Surely, I could have some time to look around beyond the hospital gates. I also ask in the email about the Czech-wolf dogs, as they are commonly used as police dogs. Even our hometown Mays Landing New Jersey has one Czech-wolf dog on the police force. I am not sure I will get a response. I will be seeing him tomorrow prior to seeing the gendarmerie and the airline investigators. I need my beauty sleep, odd how just saying every day common things bring a little sting. I set the alarm on my phone to get up before lunch time.

I get up early; shower then sit staring at Nicole's clothes. I know what I would wear if it were my clothes. Hers; not so many choices, jeans, jeans, and sweatshirts. Well, I am in a hospital for crying in a bucket, I am just gonna wear my pink gown. My head scarf I had hand washed the night before was dry and I put it on. I couldn't quite get the twisty thing going on like Greta does.

Ahh, breakfast the day's special consisted of toast, scrambled eggs, and tea. This was not bad. The hazelnut spread for the toast reminded me of Nutella.

I didn't know how long I would have to wait, so I got on my phone and checked my email and Facebook. I breezed through all of them. I constructed a general response about the sorrow and loss of my daughter and an update on my condition that was fudged in some parts. I said I had head surgery, which I did; hence the head scarf, and that my skin was damaged, which it was, and that I had lost lots of weight, which I did. I express a desire to have a memorial service when I am well enough to travel home. I tagged everyone, and included all the email addresses I had, this way everyone heard the same thing and I didn't have to remember who I told what. I sent another more personal email to my girlfriend and family, with the same update, and letting them know I was resting and getting stronger every day and not to worry about me and that I wanted to do a memorial service. I wanted the memorial service to set up in a way that gave people a chance to say good bye and share a fond memory- like a celebration of her life.

Just as I put the phone down Mary came in with a sing song cheery voice. Morning dearie, I don't often see you up this early. I brought you your blueberry muffin. Let me get you some tea. Wait, could I have coffee instead with half being milk and half coffee, like a latte. Oh, I know what you mean, I will get you one from Mila she is a barista. Thank you, Mary, you are an angel of mercy. Yep, I guess that's why I work here.

While I waited, I went into the bathroom to adjust my scarf thingy. I looked in the mirror and said, Ok girlie we have a meeting today. This is sad, weird, uncomfortable, and I can't think of any other strange words for it. What do you think? **Well mom you know how to talk, you always say talk'em till they run away.** Yep, she would say that. I smile, then try to do that smirk Nicole is so famous for, but I can't seem to get it right. Then, I realize what about all the people on the plane who won't make it home and their families.

I open the bathroom door and look over at the table to see a coffee cup alongside my blueberry muffin. The simple things in life make me happy.

Mr. Dupree knocked on the door, and said, may I come in? Yes, of course. I did get your email and I am looking into the matters. We will make sure you get a chance to see our beautiful city. Before we meet with the airline investigators and police; I wanted to give you your new passport, drivers' license and the death certificate for Nicole. Do you have your old passport and that of your daughters? Yes, I go to the closet and retrieve them and hand them over to him. Good, I will take care of them he says putting them away in his jacket pocket. Keep these out in case they wish to see them. Do you have your flight tickets as well? Yes, I retrieve them from my faithful belly bag.

Now, he says; do you have any questions for me and anything you are not sure of? I can't think of anything. Alright then, how about we get you back into bed. I know you are feeling much better, but we want them to see you still in bed recovering and maybe they won't stay as long. How are the others from the crash doing I ask? Well, most are already home, some will be here for a few more weeks, a few who will be here for months. Dr. Vinke will probably let you know soon when you can leave. I know they keep you here longer than what may seem necessary, but they want to make sure all are healed physically and have had some emotional support.

Just then, Dr. Vinke, Greta, and two other men come into my room. I am glad we are meeting here, cause Dr. Vinke's office is definitely not big enough. Dr. Vinke introduces Mr. Van de Berg from the airline and Detective Jansen. I think this is so weird but here we go.

Detective Jansen holds out his hand and says I am from the Amsterdam Koninklijke Marechaussee. I would like to ask you some questions, this is for our administrative report on the crash. Your name and whoever was traveling with you. I hand him my airline tickets, passport and my daughter's along with the death certificate, too afraid to trust my voice. He writes down all the information. The flight you were on is? It was flight 121, we were traveling here for a holiday for a once in a life time adventure. My husband died of a heart attack last year while him and my daughter were play fighting in the living room with our dog. Since it was Christmas time, I wanted us to be somewhere else for the holiday to … I am sorry that is much more than you need to know, as tears start flowing freely. Greta hands me some tissues, it's ok tears help up heal. After a few moments I am able to get control of myself. Mrs. Goodwin, on behalf of the Marechaussee we are truly sorry for the losses you have suffered. He took my hand and said we are here to help in any way; I will leave you now. I thought that was the kind of awkwardness I dread having to live through in the coming months.

Mr. Van de Berg who also looked over the documents said Mrs. Goodwin, I represent the airline, and I cannot begin to say the right words for how sorry I am that this took your daughter from you. I have some papers here that I would like for you to look over and when you are ready you can sign them or not. If you have any questions, I will leave you my card and you can call or email me.

I liked the way he said he could not begin to say the right words, because there aren't any right words. Mr. Van de Berg, thank you could you tell me the gist of the papers.

Of course, well it's basically says that all your hospital care with your case; future long term care, mental health care, flight here, costs of re-establishing yourself to return home, cost of hotel, car, clothes, technology-phones, laptops, etc... food, and first -class flight home when you are able to go. It also gives a lump sum of $100,000 for your loss and another $50,000 for yourself. It also means that if you sign you will not be able to sue the airline for damages such as wrong-full death, or pain and suffering.

Ok, I will sign it; do you have a pen?

Mr. Van de Berg says yes; I have a pen, but don't you want to read it take a few days or week to decide, it doesn't have to be signed today. Dr. Vinke and Mr. Dupree both step forward. No, it's ok, I want to move on and get this behind me. Since this will help ensure that I will have any future medical costs covered that's good enough for me. I sign all the copies. He then hands back one copy signed by him and a shiny black credit card with the airline logo. This is to cover the costs here clothing, electronics, hotel, car, food etc. When you are ready to return home, use this for your first -class flight home, the check in will then keep the card for your ticket. This is my card in case you have any questions or concerns please contact me. With that he left.

Mr. Dupree walks to my bed and says, you know you didn't have to sign today, but I will tell you that I have already read this, and it is as he says. Are you sure this about this? Yes, I said in a firm voice, I like money don't get me wrong it always helps but moving on and living this life is more important than money. I will speak to you in a few days' time. I must take my leave. He took my hand and kissed it, you are a brave and resilient woman.

Dr. Vinke came over and asked, do you have any questions or concerns? Tomorrow, I will bring you your urn of ashes as you wished. Also, today we are going to do a full head scan and testing so no physical therapy today. The orderlies will come within the next 30 minutes or so. All your testing should be done before dinner. I will make sure you get something light for lunch in between your tests. I can't imagine what this past two weeks have been like for you. You have suffered a loss, been through surgery that only a few humans ever have; that is very brave. The results of your recovery and the research are monumental with global reaching effects. You seem to have it so together.

I begin to laugh, when you're a 5th grade math teacher, you have to pretend you have it altogether all the time or they will overthrow you. We both laugh. After all your results are read Dr. Lambs and I will talk to you about your continuing care and recovery.

I am so not a fan of tests let alone brain scans or lying in claustrophobic tubes. Testing did take hours and peanut butter crackers and juice just dried out my mouth. While they wheeled me back to my room, I felt exhausted.

I got into bed and just closed my eyes, when Mary popped in. Look what I have for you for dinner! She held a pizza box. The doctor's sent it over saying they owed you. I opened it and the aroma of pepperoni and onions filled the air. Sit with me Mary. Oh no, I am too old to eat pizza. You enjoy. I did and ate the whole thing. I love pizza, and usually eat maybe two pieces, but Nicole loved pizza and could always eat a whole pie. The pizza here is so different than in America, I love the pizza here. I guess I'd better run tomorrow.

I woke up around lunch time again. I really have to start setting my alarm to get up at 6 each morning. So, today our lunch special is a ham and cheese sandwich with orange jello and tea. Mary must have the day off. I was getting used to the hospital and the people, I felt safe, I realized I didn't want to go home any time soon.

Greta came in and we walked to the flower room. I told her how I answered my email and Facebook and was taking it one day at time. Then, I said, I am afraid I will be overwhelmed when I get home. She took my hand. Lisa, there will be times you may feel overwhelmed and thinking of a way to overcome those moments is what we will talk about. The solution I had to come up with, not her helping me, was to talk in the mirror. That was my go- to strategy. I asked her to teach me how to do the twisty thing on the scarf and after 20 minutes I got it and was off to see the Punisher.

Bud was standing by the door waiting; looking at his watch. Sorry I said, I couldn't get Greta to stop talking, you know. Yea, I know he said. We are going to push you hard today. We are going to see if you can do 5 miles in 35 minutes. What! That's insane, I am a patient in a hospital who makes a patient run 5 miles. Oh, is that too hard for you? The military does forced march of a mile in 6 minutes. Ok, since you put it that way, geeze Bud, you should be in the military. I made it! I even managed to walk back to my room barely.

When I entered the room, I froze, there was a box with black ribbon. I knew exactly what it was. I did not want to open it. I put the box in the closet and closed the door.

I showered and sat in bed reading emails and Facebook. Thanked everyone for their kind words and prayers. I decided I needed rest after this long day and didn't set the alarm on my phone and was asleep within minutes.

So, I woke up at lunch time, the special was soup with crackers, lime jello, tea, and my favorite; a napkin with a blue berry muffin.

While I was practicing my scarf twisty thing, Mr. Dupree came in. Ah, Mrs. Goodwin I am glad I caught you. I wanted to give you this information and plans for your stay. First let me ask, how long do you plan on staying here? Well, when Dr. Vinke gives the ok, I was thinking about a week. Good you will time to see this beautiful city. I have an open reservation for a week at the Waldorf Astoria here, also a bike. You see most people use bikes to get around. I also have an open bus and train passes for you. I have a map of the transportation system and one of the city as well. I also made a list of the top ten places to visit. When you leave the hospital, the hotel will come and pick you up, then when you leave to go back to America the hotel will take care of the transportation to the airport. Here is the phone number for you to call. Since you are not sure when you are leaving the hospital, you will have time to map out your visit, unless you already had. You have the airline black card use that for any shopping, food, hotel stay.

Wow, this is way more than I could wish for. Thank you so much, I don't know what to say. Just say you will visit this beautiful city. I will. He took my hand in his and said in a fatherly tone, call me for anything you need.

After he left; I organized all my important documents and then sat studying the maps. All the places on Mr. Dupree's list were on the list of 20 things to do in Amsterdam. We had already mapped out each day. But I would be doing this alone. What would Nicole say? I start to get up to go to the mirror when Dr. Lambs and Dr. Vinke come into my room.

Seeing them both smiling puts me at ease. Dr. Lambs came and took my hand and said; how are you today? I feel good and even well rested from the Punisher making me do 5 miles on the treadmill yesterday. Both doctors looked at me questioningly. Oh, Bud from physical therapy, he like, you know punishes each day with hard and harder work outs. The doctors look at each other and smile. Dr. Vinke says, do you have names for us? No, no I don't, I think I said it a little too quickly because they both kept staring at me like I was lying or something.

Well, Mrs. Goodwin we have all your test results from the other day. Everything is good. We will run a few more today and I would say that you can leave the hospital the day after tomorrow. Greta has a relative in America she is contacting, a good psychiatrist for you so that you can continue with mental support. They left, and suddenly I felt I wasn't ready to leave yet.

Would people look at me with pity wearing this head scarf? Maybe I could get some kind of winter hat. I didn't even have a coat. The back packs only contain a set of clothes and pjs in case the airline lost our luggage. Greta came in smiling and I shared my concerns with her. Well, let's go shopping she said, you haven't seen our gift shop. It also has many other items, for people who don't have clothes to go home in. Get that black card Mr. Van de Berg gave you. Who doesn't like shopping?

Now, this is what gift shops should be like. Greta was right, everything you could need. I only had one jogging suit and jeans with a sweater that fit me. I got all the essentials along with new suit cases. I put my hand on Greta's arm and said, I have to pick out clothes, I don't know how to dress, it's two different generations in me. What my body is;

young in the 20's and my mind in I am in my 40's. Well, let's go for neutral and try to hit the middle. We settled on beige and black slacks with white collared button-down shirt and long-sleeved Amsterdam shirts. We also picked out a winter coat, hat and some boots since they didn't have shoes per se. Everything was well coordinated and looked great. I know I couldn't have done this by myself. Greta has great taste and an eye for fashion.

After we brought all the stuff back to my room in my new rolling suit cases, I checked the time. Oh, no, I missed physical therapy. Greta smiled and said it's ok, I texted Bud while you were paying and told him you would miss today. I do think you are having a few tests done today, so I will leave you for now and see you tomorrow. By the time I repacked everything, they came to take me for more tests. When they delivered me back to my room it was dinner time.

The day's special was a piece of chicken with salad and lime jello. As I ate, I again started to think about seeing the city alone. For the past year I have been alone except for when Nicole would come home from college or she needed me to come up and support her. We came here to get away from the sorrow of last Christmas only to suffer all over again.

I only had one more day here. Now, I would be going out into the world with a secret. My daughter is dead, and I have her body because mine was severed. How do I act like I am in my 20s? When I get home will people think I am lying, I look and sound like Nicole. Will they think I am Nicole trying to take over her mother's life? Wearing the head scarf and get some fake glasses may help. Should I just say that the hospital had to fix my skin because of burns or damage. How long should I stay out of work? What about the memorial? For the memorial I could wear a vail, it's a little bit old fashioned but some still do. My voice has Nicole's sound, but I speak like me, so maybe I could talk in a louder tone. Or just pretend like I am crying. Which I did; until sleep overtook me hours later.

I woke again at lunch time, no surprise there. Lunch special today is cheese burger with salad and lemon jello, and a wrapped blueberry muffin. Greta came in and said wow you got the scarf twist perfect. Thanks, I said, and as we walked to the flower room for the last time, I shared my thoughts from last night.

Greta looked at me for a long moment, then said, well, I am thinking since your daughter didn't wear make- up, they wouldn't recognize her if you were wearing make-up along with glasses and the head scarf you will probably wear for 6 months or get a wig. I don't think anyone would confront you on the matter, some may be wondering. I will be available for you through phone and face time for the next month we will be speaking every day. Is there anyone you trust to tell?

I was relieved to hear we would still talk every day. I thought of my friend Margaret, I could tell her. Yes, my friend, she is great at keeping secrets and is very caring. She wanted to fly here to be with me, but I had to tell her no way. Greta smiled; I am so glad you have a support when you get home. I felt much more at ease.

 I left the flower room and went to see the Punisher; it would be the last time I would see him. Hey Bud, sorry about yesterday. He looked at me; and said you look perky, let's see if we can put that perkiness to some hard work. Hard work it was I was sweaty by the time I left. I went back and showered.

I double checked that I had all my information, and everything was packed. I pulled out one of the new outfits along with the new boots. I would have to still go shopping for shoes and make up.

 I looked at my old backpack and Nicole's. The clothes didn't fit, so I put both back packs in the trash can, I wouldn't be needing them anymore.

I set the alarm to wake early and did. I got dressed in my new clothes. I also put the box with the black ribbon carefully in my new suit case. I don't know why; put I stuffed the pink gown also into my new suitcase.

Last meal and the special of the day was an egg sandwich, juice and yellow jello. I ate it all. I had just finished when Greta came in. You are up, great I want to take you somewhere before you leave. Ok, Greta where are we going? We are going to see the young girl who has your heart. She will be leaving the hospital today as well. Lisa, I have a sister in Philadelphia and she too is a psychiatrist, I know it's a drive, but I would like you to see her once a week, then once a month is that ok with you. I have contacted her already and she will be expecting a call from you. Now, let's see what your heart is up to!

Greta took my hand and we entered the room where a young girl was lying in bed. Hi, she said. Angela, I want you to meet Mrs. Goodwin whose family donated the heart. The girl was so pretty, and her eyes welled with tears as she held out both of her hands. I shakily took them into mine. She said, I am so sorry for your loss. I will take the best care and love of this heart. I am so grateful to you. I look at her for a long moment and say, love your family and cherish them EVERYDAY, because today could be the last time you can. Don't stay mad, and when you get married and have kids, hug them every day. I will she says, I promise. I realized I had met her on the plane, the girl who had to squeeze through the isle to get to the bathroom. We hugged for a long time and I kissed her on her forehead.

As we walked back to my room, we could see that both doctors were waiting for us. Dr. Lambs handed me letter and said, Mrs. Goodwin, it has been amazing to meet such a brave woman. This letter has all the information about a neurosurgeon we would like you to contact, he is my cousin. He works at the Institute of Neurology in Livingston, New Jersey. He will be expecting your call within the next 4 weeks. I also have a doctor's note for you to return to work. I have to put a date on it yet. Dr. Vinke and I think you should take 3 or 6 months before returning to work. You are physically fit, but you have had such a tragic accident that emotionally and physically getting into a routine takes time. Could you fill it out for 3 months, I don't think I could sit around the house longer than that. The doctors look at each other and shake their heads and he fills it in and hands it to me.

Dr. Vinke looks at me and put both hands on top of my shoulders. Mrs. Goodwin, your test results came back again all normal. If you have any problems or questions you call. All your paperwork and contact info for myself and Dr. Lambs is included; is at the nurse's desk ready for you to take with you. You have been one of the most amazing patients and the research from your surgery is going to affect many in the future. I hug him tightly and say, you saved us I will always be grateful to you to my whole life. Then I hug Dr. Lambs and tell them thank you for all that you have done for me. Greta looks at me with tears in her eyes, I am not supposed to cry, but I will miss seeing you every day, and we will talk every day. I hug her the longest. I know, I say, I will call you.

Mr. Dupree who was standing behind the doctors came forward. Mrs. Goodwin, I wanted to be here to take you to the hotel myself. Ok, everybody has to go because this is getting too teary eyed. Mr. Dupree picks up my suitcase and we walk to the nurse's station and sign the release papers. I turn and look at him for a moment, thank you so much for coming to get me.

As we go through the hospital doors, he turns to me and says, ok it's time for an adventure. I freeze for a moment at his words. He stops and looks concerned, are you alright? Yes, I say slowly, a new life and new adventure. I suppose people who come close to death experience some type of renewed spirit or life. I smile at him, and I couldn't have started it without the kindest person I know. It started snowing by the time we reached his car. The drive won't take long, but I will take you around the hotel so you can see what you are near and get a lay of the land. He gives me the history the and sightseeing tour for well over two hours. He explains how the trains run and shows me how to find them and the bus stops. By the time we drive up to the hotel it's dark. We enter a beautiful lobby and walk to the front desk. Good evening Mr. Dupree, we have all the arrangements you requested. Here is the key to your suite number 1019. If you should need anything, please just pick up the phone. As we walk to the elevators, I say, there is no need for you to come up. I am on my new adventure. I reach over and hug him. Just then the elevator opens I take my suitcase and go in. He says, call me for anything you need and waves.

When I find the room and enter, my breath is taken away. This was the most beautiful room I had ever seen. Yea, this wasn't on our original budget plan. This is like an apartment, a living room, a wet bar area, a space to have 6 to 8 people dining room table, another area with a desk, a bed room, a closet the size of a bedroom and not just a bathroom, a Jacuzzi pool thingy. Ok, so I jumped on the bed then swung my arms around and danced a little in each room. I put my suitcase in the bedroom and unpacked. I didn't have much. I put the box with the black ribbon on the table, next to my bed. I sat looking at it, and thought, most of that is me, and just Nicole's brain. It's both of us.

I showered and changed. It was dark out and still snowing. I decided to have dinner, room service, I had a big enough table for it. I went to the foyer and found the menu. I sat on the bed and studied it carefully. I didn't want to be pig, but it all looked so good. I could see myself ordering everything like those commercials. I finally settled on pepperoni pizza and café latte with some stroopwafel.

When I finished, I laid out my clothes for the next day with maps and a list of places I wanted to go; near the hotel. I went into the bathroom and looked into the mirror. Ok, we have got to stop eating all this pizza, we are going to eat like the locals tomorrow. I tried to smirk, but it still didn't look right. **Ok, mom no talking to strangers.** Ok, Nicole I will play it safe. I blew her a kiss and went to bed early.

The bed was so comfortable, no, unbelievably comfortable, like it was for a king, or queen. I never slept go peacefully in all my life. I woke early and laid in the bed for over an hour relishing in comfort. I decided room service for breakfast, scrambled eggs, sausage and toast with jam and café latte. Once ordered, I got dressed and packed all the maps and list up in my belly bag. I would get a purse and go shopping while I saw the sights. I stood by the window and saw that it was cloudy but looked like a good day. There was a knock at the door. After eating the fluffiest scrambled eggs, I literally wiped the plate clean with the toast to get it all. That's when I realized I hadn't said good bye to Mary at the hospital. I would pick up a gifts for them and send them over to the hospital.

I was ready to start my day, my adventure. I would use my phone for picture taking. When I walked outside, the sun was making its way out of the clouds. It was only 40 degrees. With all the walking I was planning; this would be great weather. I wanted to see the museums first and they weren't that far from each other, so, I would start there, and a visit to the gift shops. At the Van Gogh and Stedelijk museums I not only spent hours in, but the gift shops were a mine field. I picked up a beautiful scarf for Greta and a warm well -made sweater for Mary. I found some beautiful made wooden clogs for my friend Margaret. I also got a small photo for sister and boxes of Puccini bomboni for her and my brothers which I decided to have mailed home as this all would not fit in my bags.

After the museums I started walking to find gifts for the doctors and Bud. I took out my map to see where I was. I was starting to get hungry. I saw a little restaurant across the street and decided to go. I was so little and quaint. I ordered a broodje kroket (deep fried meat ragout croquette on a soft bun) and water. Well, the food it good, different from what I am used to, but the food has a blend of flavors which makes it so enjoyable.

After lunch, I decided to start heading back towards the hotel. Now, I really enjoyed the view, before I was busy just looking for street names that I didn't enjoy the view. Such a wonderful old city with bridges to cross. I saw a cheese shop; and in the window was a guillotine cheese slicer. Oh yeah, that I was getting that for Bud the Punisher, with a few blocks of cheese.

I made my way back to the hotel and decided to stop in the gift shop. Wow, the clothes and make up was to die for. Yep, I went crazy at the cosmetics and toilettes and bought 5 more outfits and lacey underclothes and pjs, I don't think they call them pjs, but they were so soft and pretty. I saw the most modest looking bath-suit and running outfit I just had to get. I bought a beautiful purse with matching scarf, mirror, and wallet. I picked out matching wrapping & writing paper. Then I saw a counter with pens and watches. There was the most delicate woman's watch with tulips and diamonds. It cost what I make in a month, but I just really wanted it. I picked out three Monte Blanc pens and had them engraved with the doctors' names and one for Mr. Dupree.

Well, the only thing I really needed were shoes. I couldn't wear Nicole's sneakers with the clothes, and the boots weren't really fashionable. Tomorrow I would look for some shoe stores.

I called Greta and told her all about my hotel room and food, and the broodje kroket I had eaten. I told her my plan to find some shoes and that I was doing ok. She was pleased and reminded me to call again tomorrow.

I put on the new running outfit and decided to check out the gym. What a gym it was, not like the hospital at all. This was like something you would see for fitness gurus. I started on the treadmill with the TV screen that let you pick a scene to walk or run. I picked the jungle one with a tiger chasing me. After 40 minutes, the tiger still hadn't caught me, so I left the jungle. I wanted to see the pool area and that was just as incredible. I was tired and went back to my room.

Tonight, I would sit in the Jacuzzi spa they call it. It was written on the side. I would order room service and send off some emails and download my pictures I had taken; to the Google site Nicole and I set up before the trip, for photos. We were not to face the same direction when taking pictures so we could have twice as many different views. She was a smart cookie my kid.

After finishing dinner of steak and salad with a café latte and a blueberry muffin, I wrapped the gifts and wrote thank you notes to everyone. I have spent the last few weeks with these people during a horrific experience. Their kindness, calm, and insight have helped me from losing my mind and helped me put my life into perspective. I was still me, just a new body, or younger body, but I am ME.

The next day I awoke to a shining sun. I knew exactly what I would have for breakfast, the same, it was so good. I knew I had to get shoes, but I also thought, I need to replace the laptop that I lost in my luggage. Using the phone for emails and such was so cumbersome. That was my plan of action today. I looked up computer stores and shoe stores. I kinda felt guilty all the money I am spending on this credit card but if they balked, I could use the money they would give me to offset the costs.

The computer store was the first stop. They brought out a top of the line laptop with all the essentials and then some. There were some many boxes, for wireless mouse, pen, cords for printing, for casting, for this and that. When it was all wrapped up, I didn't know how I would carry it all. The gentleman behind the counter saw me trying to clutch all the packages and had pity on me. Ma'am where are you staying. I told him and he smiled. I will contact their concierge and they will come and get it for you. Great. Wow I wish every store had this. He gave me a signed receipt and I left.

Now, to find shoes or lunch. I had been in the store almost three and half hours. I would hop on the bus with the ticket I had and go close to the shoe shop and look for places to eat. I took pictures out the window, how touristy I thought.

When I got off the bus, there was the shoe shop but also some food places. Humm would my feet be fatter after I ate? I went into the shoe shop first. As I was looking at the shoes in the window, I heard a familiar voice. Lisa in the jogging suit. I turned and smiled, hey Thijs with the cool name. What are you doing here? This is my parent's shop, I to work here and am apprentice. Oh, you make shoes here. Yes, and I will find the best pair for you. Ok then, I am a size 8, I am looking for something comfortable and classic that will go with everything. Ahh, you want one with a heel for your classic and small heel for comfortable walking. Sounds perfect. He turned and left to go into the back. His mother, I guessed, came out, and I said hello. I asked if she was the one who made the pea soup. Her eyes lit up, yes, I did. Oh, I said that was the best pea soup I have ever had. You must be the girl from the hospital. No, I thought the older woman not the 20-year-old. Now this was getting awkward. People didn't see me, the 40 something old math teacher, they saw a beautiful young 20 something single girl. Yes, I met your son at the hospital where your daughter works.

After an hour of trying on shoes and finding not two, but four pairs I really liked, I paid for my shoes. I asked Thijs where I could find some great places to eat. His mother on hearing this, said "Oh Thijs take Lisa out and show her the city and go to the café for lunch". Oh, I don't want to be a bother I say hoping he would not. Ok mama, I will be back in a couple of hours. Yikes, I thought what I should do now. Thijs took my bags of shoes and we were off.

We walked for about an hour with Thijs giving me the history tour of each and every building we passed. Then we went into a little café with a coffee shop attached. Now, most tourist learn quickly that a coffee shop is also a pot shop, not like in America. You can get high just sitting in one. And we did, but at least we had lunch to stave off the munchies. I am not big on sausage sandwich, but this was incredible. As I began to really relax, due to the smoky air. Thijs told me how he was working with his parents, and went to college, and his girlfriend was away on holiday. Thank goodness I thought. He wanted to know if I would tell him all about America, as he wanted to take his girlfriend. Well, I think I will have another sausage sandwich, and we did. I told him all about America, Disney, and the cities he should visit. After two hours; I stumbled out of the café; he had more experience than I did.

We walked for another half an hour with commentary until we were in front of the bus stop and next to his shop. My mother is having a big dinner tomorrow at 4:00 because my sister has the day off and they do lots of cooking all day, you must come, please. Yea, I would love to. You're right next to the bus stop, I can do that. The bus pulled up and I got my ticket out, he handed me my bags and we waved good bye.

I am so glad for buses because there was no way I could walk straight back to the hotel in my condition. The bus stopped in front of the hotel and I got off. I walked, if you could call it that, across the street to sit on one the benches overlooking the cannel.

I got out my phone for more pictures and called Greta. I told her about my day and yes, the visit to the coffee shop, she laughed. I told her about the awkwardness with Thijs and how relieved I was that he had a girlfriend. I said, being in my forties I figured I had another 40 years left in life, now I am in a 20-year body I have some 60 years left. Men would look at me and see a 20 something girl. She asked me how I felt about that, I told her I am not sure yet and would talk to her tomorrow.

I got up with my bags and went into the hotel. I went straight into the gift shop and looked at rings. I found a simple diamond and band that was so beautiful in its simplicity I bought it and put it on. When my husband had died last year, I put my rings in his casket, and Nicole put her favorite story book that he had read to her nightly until she was 13.

I went upstairs to my room and found all my computer boxes neatly stacked on the desk. Wow this is great service. I put on my new bathing suit and went swimming in the hotel pool. As I rested in the hot water area, I thought about how I was so outgoing and talked to everyone. Yet; now I find myself being hesitant. Why? Was it because now people saw me as a young girl, and not an older woman? Should my usual friendliness be tampered with how I look if I am talking to men or boys? Would they take it the wrong way, like I did with Thijs? He wasn't acting different; but I was taking it the wrong way. Will I sound like a know it all when talking to young people, if they see me as a young person? If I speak to older people in their 40s my age, how will they perceive me? This was so much to think about, my head started to hurt. I am now the new social awkward female. Am I a woman, or girl? Will I shop in the Women's section of clothes or the Misses'? I laughed out loud and a few people looked at me strangely, yep it's just me the social awkward female.

I left the pool and returned to my room and showered then put on my new jammies. My used clothing was piling up. Why not, I took the laundry cleaning bag out and put what I needed clean in it and hung it on my door. Now, what to do for dinner. I decided on crab cocktail, lobster bisque, and a Caesar with anchovies and chocolate ice cream.

After I finished dinner; I set up my new laptop. I sent new email updates and Facebook updates. Texting and email were easy, but I had to at one-point talk to my family and Margaret, and they would hear Nicole's voice. Greta and I talked about this, me using a louder tone and my personality would come through. Maybe it would work, but Margaret and I have been friends since birth. I would tell her when I see her. In my email I asked her how Bella, my giant poodle, was doing and laughed at the pictures she had sent. I told her I would be coming home in about 4 days, but I didn't want anyone at all to know. I told her I wanted her to pick me up at the airport. She must promise me she wouldn't tell anyone that I was coming home. I also asked what she thought about doing the memorial for Nicole; again. I closed the laptop and went to bed.

Ahh the next morning I just lay in bed. I have never fell in love with a bed, but I am in love with this bed. I ordered breakfast, the same. Most people eat the same thing every day for breakfast, maybe not a hotel like this though. I hope they don't think I am licking the plate. I left some crumbs just in case.

I got dressed in my new clothes and shoes. The shoes were well made and soft leather and water proof which was important. The hair on my head was growing fast and starting to stick up all over. There was still the red ugly scar from one ear to the other ear, but the hair was tall enough to cover most of it. I would have to ask the doctor when I could dye my hair. When I had hit the age of 38 the grays were coming hard and fast. I had started dying my hair and knew I was a Paul Mitchell 6C color. Wearing the head scarf made me feel safe, even though people would stare.

As I entered the lobby, I detoured into the gift shop. I really have to stop this; I know where everything is in this shop and they know my first name. Sun glasses galore. I chose the 'Whitney' polarized sunglasses and was off for some more touristy things.

I started with a canal cruise. The boat was not only heated but served wine. Well, I got nice and toasty. The boat then let off near the Ons' Lieve Heer op Solder museum which was on my list. It was already one o'clock. I needed something light to eat as I was going to Thijs's house at four. I saw a pancake shop and a 'coffee shop', Humm, I choose the 'coffee shop' and maybe stayed a little longer than was necessary.

I sat on a bench drinking hot chocolate and decided to call Greta and tell her about my day and new sunglasses. She asked me if I normally wore sunglasses, I said yes, as my light blue eyes tear up in bright sun. Greta I will never look at another coffee shop the same way when I get back to America, we both laughed. I told her that I was having dinner with a family whose daughter worked at the hospital and the mother had sent jars of pea soup whose name I couldn't pronounce. Greta knew of whom I spoke and asked in a firm voice; how are you coping Lisa? There was silence on the phone for less than a minute, I managed to find my voice and say, one day at a time. Even though I can see her and hear her; I miss her.

I sat watching people on bikes, boats, walkers, and life just going by, like everything is the same still. I didn't know what stage of grief I was in, but every time I would look in the mirror, I would miss her. My heart ached in pain when I thought of my precious baby girl. I was afraid I would start blubbering, so I got up and searched for the bus.

I got to Thijs's house a little after four o'clock and it was time to eat. Thijs's parents, sister, her boyfriend, and their elderly neighbors sat around the overflowing table of food. There was Haring 'Hollandse Nieuwe', Krokets, Poffertjes, Bitterballens, Oliebollen, and Erwtensoep soup. I have never eaten so many different kinds of food. I almost ate all the Bitterballens before I came to my senses and realized that there are other people at the table who might like some. Awkward moment, I had counted how many I ate and realized I had eaten about four persons' share. When the slowing down of food intake came, Thijs's sister Mila asked me to tell them all about America. Well, the first thing I want you to know about America is they don't have the great food like you have here. Everyone laughed and desserts and coffee flowed freely for over four hours. It was getting late and I needed to catch the bus which would be coming in 15 minutes. I stood and looked at everyone, I want to thank you for inviting me into your home to share this wonderful meal with family and neighbors. I lost a loved one in the plane crash it's been hard to see life. Tonight, you have all helped me see that being loved, happy, and together to celebrate LIFE is what I need to see. There were tears in the women's eyes and dampness in the men's eyes. Thank you so much for tonight it means so much to me. Then the tears started falling and a few coughs. I also, want to apologize to my host for eating almost all the Bitterballens. Laughing all around broke the sorrow of the moment, and I took my leave.

I got back to the hotel and was restless. I called the front desk and asked about sending packages to the hospital and one to the American Embassy. The woman told me a porter would come up to retrieve the packages and they would be sent tomorrow by messenger. I thank her profusely. I hope she didn't think I was crazy, but here you're not crazy; just in the "coffee shop" mode, I suppose. Within a few minutes a bell boy came and took the packages which I had already addressed. Do they have this in America I wondered?

I opened my laptop and sent Dr. Vinke an email asking when I could safely dye my hair. I sent another to Mr. Dupree saying that I would be leaving in two days and thanking him for all his help. I didn't want to forget what I ate tonight, so I made a note of it on my computer. I also created an email to Greta saying I can't say the names of all the food I ate but here is the list. I shut off my laptop and sat on the bed.

I dressed in running clothes and went down to the gym. I wanted to try the mountains with a mountain lion chasing me. I supposed all the food slowed me down because after 30 minutes I had to get off as the mountain lion almost got me. I went back to my room and showered and changed. I really love these pjs.

I picked up the box with the black ribbon. Should I? Shouldn't I? I opened the box to find a large sheer red ribbon wrapped around a heart shaped urn. My daughter's name, birth date, death date and a beautiful angel with her wings spread and her hands held together holding a star. I was so touched by the kindness I was speechless and teary eyed. I put the urn on the bedside table and slept.

I woke at 3:00 am. Something was not right. I turned on the lights and went straight for the mini-bar and found some rum and Coke. I poured myself a stiff drink, and then another; because I needed it for what I was about to do.

I sat at the desk and turned on the laptop. I found the video-call icon and click it. I put in Margaret's number and waited. It would only be 9:00 pm there. When her face came on the screen, there was a split second of shock registered in her eyes; then it was gone. It's me, Lisa, I have something to tell you before I come home, because it will be a shock to you.

After three hours, the sun was coming through my windows. Margaret was still a little teary eyed. I need you to be strong for me I said. I wanted you to understand why I didn't want to see anyone when I came home. Ok, Lisa, this is a lot to take in, you know I will do my best in anything you need me to do. I need understanding and a shoulder from you, I said. Also, on a happier note I have a couple of recipes I would love for you to make, I already sent them to your in-box. She smiled, oh, a happier note; I do the all the cooking! Well, you are the better cook!

After I closed my laptop, I sat and stared at the wall. Would our friendship feel different when we saw each other in person? I already felt a little weird when she stared at me, trying to believe it was me and not Nicole. I had to tell her secrets in detail only her and I knew. We won't see each other as the same I thought.

I ordered breakfast, the same and really enjoyed the meal. I did leave some crumbs on the plate. Then I showered and dressed for the day. I only had today and tomorrow. I turned on my laptop and searched for flights. I found one that would be non-stop night flight for the day after tomorrow. I booked it first class. I sent all the information to Mr. Dupree,

Greta, Dr. Lambs, Dr. Vinke, and Margaret. I also arranged for a car to take me to the airport.

I found a few emails. One from Dr. Vinke, he said I should wait at least 60 days before dying my hair. I wrote thank you emails again to all of them. They would be getting their gifts today I thought. I began laughing thinking about Bud opening his.

Today would be a picture-perfect day, because I planned on taking lots of pictures. I took a pizza canal tour and it was worth it. I visited the Oude Kerk church, Nieuwe Kerk, Moses and Aaron, and the Ons'Lieve Heer op Solder church. I had taken over 450 pictures just this day. I was filled with awe at the history and beauty of these treasured places.

It was getting late, so I called Greta and told her all the places I had already seen today. I told her I was so tired and resting on a bench. She reminded me to make sure that I called her tomorrow. I promised I would. I hadn't stopped for lunch and was getting quite hungry. I stopped at the Ciel Blue and ordered the Saint-Tropez. I took some pictures and a few people stared at me. I guess people in this kind of place don't take pictures, too bad. What a view and what an experience. This was a once in a life time adventure.

I strolled the streets in the direction of the closest bus stop. Walking is the only way to truly see the city and the people. Most people would give me a sad smile, thinking I had cancer because of the head scarf.

I stopped at a store that had wines. I wanted to send something to Thijs's family, and I knew they loved wine. I bought four bottles of their best and well yea, the most expensive. I left the store and sat down on a bench next to the bus stop. My ring was sparkling in the sun sending little rays of light.

When I made it back to the hotel, I was so tired. I glanced in the direction of the gift shop, then looked away, then turned around and walked in. I decided a woman can never have enough make-up. I didn't wear cover-up or face base, but I wanted to try it out. After getting another cosmetic bag to hold all the new make-up I walked over to the jewelry counter. I saw the most beautiful tulip opal earrings. Opal was Nicole's birthstone. The price tag was almost two of my paychecks. But I got them anyway. Still tired, I decided to pick up some more under-clothes. Then, I dragged myself into the elevator.

I unpacked everything and wrapped the wine and wrote a long heart-felt thank you note. I called the concierge about having it delivered. Then, I got into the Jacuzzi spa and fell asleep for over an hour. When I woke in cool water, I got out and changed into pjs. It was getting late, but I was hungry. I ordered lobster bisque and shrimp cocktail. When the bell hop came with my late-night dinner, he also took my package. I sat in bed while I ate, knowing I would have to leave this bed behind. This was my last night, because tomorrow night I would be boarding a plane for home, alone.

I woke the next day and just laid in bed. I ordered breakfast and ate it in bed. This time I did wipe the plate clean. It was a cloudy day. I didn't even feel like getting up. I took out my mirror and stared at my daughter's reflection for a long time. I hadn't really thought about the young girl who had my heart. I prayed to the Lord, that she would get a long life. That heart had been through a lot, more joy than anything else and I hoped that would be the same for her.

Why me, why Nicole, why this young girl? I could feel anger rising in me, and I knew it wasn't fair, why did I have to lose a husband and a daughter? Over the years teaching; I saw many families' lives get shattered in various ways. I had come to believe a few things that made sense to me. It doesn't matter why or how, it's *what will you do now*. Events in life can make you *bitter* or *better*, choose.

● ● ●

Finally, I heard Nicole's voice, **"Come on, lazy bones you're wasting a day!"** I smiled at her reflection and said, I will do my best baby girl.

I got out of bed and showered and changed. I packed all the new things I had bought and laid out all the important documents and passport and packed them into my purse. I went to the window and could see that it was beginning to snow. I pulled a chair up to the window so I could be right next to it. I phoned Greta.

I told Greta, I missed the flower room and her too. She thanked me for the gift and thanked me for the beautiful thank you note. She sounded like she was maybe crying. I told her that I had called Margaret the other day and explained the donor surgery. Margaret knew me and understood what I had done and would have done the same. Margaret will be there for me. Greta said she was so glad I had someone I could trust with my feelings. I asked, Greta, when I Margaret, I will see my friend, but what will she see? That is a question you will have to explore with your friend. I guess so. Maybe she will be jealous of my cute body. Greta laughed, then said, you will get through this and I believe you are much stronger than most. Call me Lisa, when you get home. I will, thank you for believing in me.

As I stared out the window the snow continued to fall. It doesn't really snow a lot in January, but it was today. It was past lunch time, so I ordered a sausage sandwich and chocolate ice-cream. After finishing the lunch, I got onto my laptop and sent email updates to family and friends and Facebook. I saw thank you emails from Dr. Lambs and Dr. Vinke. Dr. Vinke said that Mary cried when she opened her gift. I also emailed my principal and told her that I would be back to work around April. I had the doctor's note and sent her a picture of it. I also, explained that I had doctors' appointments weekly and that when I came home, (I didn't tell her when) I would have to continue seeing various doctors in America and would be ready to work in April. I felt guilty, even though I didn't lie per se, I didn't tell her everything.

I packed up the laptop and the boxed the urn; then went to sit by the widow again. The snow was still falling. I jumped up out of the chair and went down stairs and out the doors. I turned towards the hotel to see where my room window was and went across the street and lay down on the sidewalk and made a snow angel. I was so glad the snow was dry and not wet. I got up and looked at my snow angel, just like the one Nicole had made the day we left. I went back inside the hotel, traipsing in snow, and got some frowns from people checking in. I made my way quickly to the elevators and got into my room. I raced to the window and looked out. There was my snow angel.

While I sat looking out the window, a loud knock on the door startled me. I went to the door, hoping I wasn't in trouble for the snow I trailed in. The bell boy had a package. Ma'am this was delivered for you. Thank you and closed the door. The box was wrapped in brown paper. I pulled the note from under the string and read it. It was from Thijs's mother. She made me 3 dozen Bitterballens and they were packed in dry ice and would stay frozen for over 30 hours. She ended the note with well wishes and that she hoped I would return in the future as their home welcomes me. I put the package in my suitcase. I was so glad to have two attachable-wheeled suitcases and I still had some room left in one of them.

I called to confirm the transportation pick-up and pre-flight check in. All was set. I would be leaving soon. Well, I am going to have dinner in bed. What to order for my last dinner here? I decided on pepperoni pizza with onions a chocolate shake, strawberry cake. The best part was eating in bed. I thought about it and wondered if I would have let Nicole eat dinner in bed. I only had an hour before leaving.

• • •

Five minutes before transportation was to arrive, I went to the lobby to wait. I suppose most well-to-do people would be in their rooms and couldn't be bothered to bring their luggage down. Not me, my father always taught me, "Do it yourself because nobody else wants to".

I thought about how I had been feeling that life goes on around you as if nothing ever happened to me. I had felt that way when my husband died. Everybody went on as usual as if the event never happened. Focus on life and the living and what you want to make it. Celebrate life and those that are not here and with those that are here now with you. Celebrate your family and friends with joy and love. Even though I had lost two of my family, my whole family, I knew I didn't want to sink into depression, because I felt too weak to get myself out.

I felt I had to call Greta, so I did. I told her I was waiting to go to the airport. Greta, I know some questions can only be answered as time passes. When I opened my eyes after the crash, and was in the hospital, I panicked wondering if Nicole was alright. When Dr. Vinke told me, she was brain dead I begged him to put my brain into her body because she was too young to die. Did I do this to save myself or her? After what seemed like an eternity of silence, Greta said in a firm voice, I believe you chose

• • •

to save both of you. Greta you are an angel, I will talk to you when I get home, but remember the time differences and hung up. I looked at my phone, and it seemed like someone else had called me. Well, they will call back. I could see the driver heading towards me.

As we got into the car, I looked across the street at my snow angel, it was still there. The snow had stopped, and I was on my way home. When we got to the airport it started snowing heavily. I went to the counter to retrieve my ticket and gave him the airline black credit card. The man behind the counter took it, then look at me. His eyes conveyed sorrow, and tears welled up in my eyes. He turned to another young man behind him and tilted his head toward me. The young man came around the counter, I will take your luggage and put it on the plane for you by your seat. There is a waiting area over here for you to sit until we take off in about 65 minutes. I pulled myself together, knowing that I was getting stares from the people behind me. I supposed they thought I was sick, seeing the head scarf, I said to myself. I followed him into the waiting area. This wasn't a real waiting area I thought. There was a bar with a bartender, a buffet table, leather seating, couches. Ok, since this is the first and last time, I will ever afford first-class, this is quite an experience, and disappointment the next time I fly anywhere. There were only a few people. I wanted pictures but I had to do it casually, so I pretended I was looking for a signal on my phone. This was, my once in a life time adventure after all. I went to the bar, what the heck, got a double. I went over to the buffet and what to my wondering eyes did see but; Bitterballens. I filled a plate with them, not caring if anyone thought me greedy.

When I plopped the last one in my mouth, I thought about getting up and getting more. No, I had better not, I ate almost all of them. I sat and sipped my double which tasted like a triple. The door to the waiting area opened loudly and I turned as everyone else did to see Mr. Dupree entering. A couple of men waved and said greetings to him. When he saw me; he walked over to me carrying a box.

I tried calling you, but maybe not so good phone reception. He put the box down at my feet. I wanted to first thank you for the note and the gift, it was not necessary for you to get such a beautiful gift, it will be well used. Thank you, Mr. Dupree, for all your kindness and support, I don't know what I would have done without you. He removed an envelope from his jacket pocket and handed it to me. Put these papers in your purse for safe keeping. I did so, confused. Then he pulled from his coat pocket a bottled water and a fabric bowl which he put beside my purse. He looked at me and said, I wanted to make sure you had everything before you left. I hope that one day you will come again happier to the city.

With that said, he opened the box, to reveal a sleeping puppy wrapped in a pink blanket. I was speechless, I lifted the puppy into my arms and could hear her quietly snoring. Thank you doesn't seem enough for the bundle of joy you have given me. Mr. Dupree petted the puppy's head; I didn't want you to travel home alone. Miss puppy has all her shots and chipped and pedigree papers which I gave you, along with travel papers. The vet sedated the her, and she should sleep for the next 10 to 15 hours which gives you enough time to get home. She may wake up groggily and will most likely fall back asleep. She needs a name. I don't know what to say. He laughed and said Greta, I mean, Ms. Homestead, thought it was a great idea. Just then, an announcement came on that boarding would commence in 5 minutes. Mrs. Goodwin, it has been a pleasure to meet you, I am sorry that it wasn't under happier circumstances. I had better go. I hugged him for a long moment. He turned and waved good bye.

Now, everyone was staring at me holding a puppy. Awkward moment. I put the puppy back into the box and grabbed my purse and headed out to my flight. At the door was a flight attendant who showed me to my seat, well not just a seat, a lounge chair really, in leather with a table and cup holders attached. I got my phone out to take more pictures. So, what, I am a tourist! It's a once in a life time adventure.

During the flight, I texted Margaret again to let her know what time the plane would land and that the gentleman from the American Embassy had given me a gift. I picked up the puppy and put her head on my shoulder. During the flight the puppy woke, and sleepily looked at me, then she licked my face and put her head back down and went to sleep. What will I call you? You were supposed to be Nicole's dog. I thought about Bella at home, what would she think of me? I would be acting like me, but looking, sounding, and smelling like Nicole. She would only put her head on my shoulder and snuggle against my neck. Bella did love Nicole and my husband but only me did she snuggle with. I decided the Max would fit. So Max, I said quietly, you will meet a new friend; Bella.

As I sat there, or rather lay as I had the seat extended, I thought; what will it be like going into my home. I have to get used to a new life, a new me, what?

PART 2

When it was time to exit the plane, I put Max back into the box, and grabbed my purse. The flight attendant took my luggage from a closet and said, please follow me. We took a shortcut to the exit area of the airport. He hand me the handle of my luggage. Have a nice day ma'am. Wow, now that was a miracle! I could see Margaret reading the leader board for flight information. I walked over to her, and at first, she didn't recognize me. Hey stranger, do I get a welcome home? She looked at me with a smile in her eyes and hugged me for a long very long time. I lifted the box and said look at the gift I got. She opened it and looked in. She made a humming sound and snatched up the puppy. Hey, you can take my luggage, I get the puppy, now give her back. We laughed and made the exchange. On the way home I told her about my experience with first class waiting area and seating.

We were home within 15 minutes, and since it was night time most of the neighbors were sleeping. I really didn't want to do any greetings. Margaret put my suitcases upstairs, I asked her to open them and get the brown papered box and bring it downstairs.

A few minutes later she came down with the box. Well, well, well, I like your new wardrobe. I laughed and took the box from her. I unwrapped it and explained what it was. I took out a few and put the rest away. I microwaved them and we ate them. So, I said, this is what your new receipt should taste like. I am expecting you to make this on my birthday, and any holiday events you invite me to. Now that I think of it, this box will probably be finished with a week, which should give you enough time to make some for taste testing, right.

We went into the living room where the puppy lay on the floor sleeping. Margaret said, I will bring Bella over later today, I didn't want to bring her to the airport in case she had sit in the car to long. That's fine I said. It will give me time to unpack and get settled before she comes home. I want to be able to properly introduce her new friend.

We sat quietly watching the puppy snore. I looked at Margaret and said, tell me what you think. She looked up and sat quiet for a moment before speaking. My heart is heavy for the loss of Nicole. Seeing you, or her body and voice, I don't feel as sad, it's like she is here somehow. The way you talk to me is you and I feel like you are here with me too. It is better than having just one or just the other. It's the best of both of you. It's like you are both still here. Ok, so if I didn't tell you about the donor swap, would you think I am me or Nicole acting like me. Margaret took a moment before answering. I knew she was really thinking about an honest answer. When I first saw you at the airport, I saw the head scarf and you were wearing makeup and the clothes were your style, so, yea, I did see you. I knew she had given me the answer I needed, but it was also her honest answer to what she saw. I know you mean it Margaret, and I am so relieved. It has been my biggest fear that people will think I am lying and that I am Nicole trying to pull off being her mother. No, I don't see that at all. Nicole didn't wear make-up or glasses, hey where are your glasses? I have 20/20 now, so I was thinking about picking up a fake pair of glasses. That sounds weird. We both laugh. Thanks, Margaret for being a great friend and an angel. Now, you aren't jealous of my body, are you? Now, she threw the couch pillows at me.

She left and promised to bring Bella around noon time to give me time to unpack and take a nap. I unpacked the Christmas ornament and put it downstairs in the basement with all the other ones she had made for the past 23 years. I took Max with me upstairs to my bed room and we both took a nap for the next 5 hours.

I woke to find Max licking my face. Her eyes were wide awake. I said, ok Max let's take you outside for pee-pee. I don't know if Max had to go really bad or just listened well, but as soon as I put her down, she squatted down and went. We had three more hours until Margaret would bring Bella home. I set out a bowl of water and food and put Max in front of it. She was thirsty. I decided to let her get a chance to smell out her new home and Bella's domain. I went to my closet, yikes, none of these clothes fit me. I got a large garbage bag and literally put all my clothes including under clothes, and pjs in, except for the black dress I wore for my husband's funeral. I put my new clothes in. The closet still seemed empty. I brought the two large clothes bags down and put them on the front porch. Then sat down on the bottom step. I would do Nicole's room another day. I also had to clean out her dorm room at college. I had to plan her memorial. I had doctor's appointments to make. I was glad that the doctor gave me at least three months before returning to work.

Max was playing with one of Bella's stuffed toys. When I called Max, she looked up and with the toy still in her mouth came running. I played with her and when I couldn't take it anymore, picked her and squeezed her tightly to me. Ok, Max I think another potty stop. This time I let her follow me outside to the potty pen; I called it. We walked down the side walk, she sniffed the dirt and went both. Now, let's see if you can keep up this excellent behavior up. She looked up at me, and I couldn't resist. You are so stinking cute. You will probably never learn to run because I will always be carrying you. We went back inside.

It was almost noon, so I ordered a couple of chicken Caesar salads. I didn't know if Max had ever walked on a lease or not but gave it go. Since the sub shop where I ordered was only a block away, I took Max. Everyone in the store, welcomed me back and gave condolences. It was sad to see how they struggled to find the right words, because there really aren't any right words. We walked back home just as Margaret was pulling up. I handed her the salads and was knocked over by Bella. She was so happy her little knob tail wagged so fast you could hardly see it. I wondered for a second, who she thought I was. That's when her new friend jumped onto my chest. Bella was as surprised as I was. Bella and Max sniffed. Bella could already smell the puppy's scent on me. Max already knew it was Bella's home. The dance began. Bella started turning around in circles with joy, and Max trying unsuccessfully to jump up on her. As Margaret and I went into the house the dogs followed.

We just sat; ate our lunch watching the dogs. Margaret looked at me and said, what's in those garbage bags on your porch? Well, I unpacked my suitcases and the clothes in my closet don't fit me anymore. Oh, I can take them for you and drop them off at the donation bin, I have to go shopping anyway. Thanks, it would really help. I think I may need your help when I do Nicole's room. Sure, I can help.

So, Margaret how about we have Nicole's memorial in about a month. I would like to just be home and give myself some time alone. I already told the principal that I wasn't coming back until April. I have doctors' visits I have to make and travel to. I can't dye my hair, much of what there is, for 60 days, so I will be wearing this head scarf until then. I have to clean out Nicole's dorm room at college as well. Margaret took my hand, no worries, I already started planning the memorial service. I have of list of her friends and those from college and high school, and I started a Facebook page memorial for her, so we can update people about the memorial. Now, what do you want to do? Margaret I just want to get over this jet lag and time difference.

The dogs were done play wrestling. I'd better let the dogs out in the back yard. I scooped up the puppy for a little squeeze and opened the door for them to go out. It was a warm January day about 43 degrees so they would be fine outside.

I came back into the living room where Margaret sat staring at me as I entered the room. What, I said. Ok, so is it weird living in your daughter's body. Like when guys look at you, when you go to the bathroom, stupid stuff I don't know what I am saying. I laughed at her. I held out my hand so she could see the rings on it. Whoa, what is this? I explained how I met this young man at the hospital, and how at first, I thought he was interested in me, and it made me feel weird. I couldn't imagine kissing someone with my daughter's lips. I was saved when he told me he had a girlfriend; he was more interested in hearing about America because he wanted to take his girlfriend there. Yea, I picked up the rings, so guys won't bother me. I don't know how I would feel getting involved with a man, kissing, or having sex with a man in my daughter's body. If my body was another woman's body, I guess I would be ok with finding a boyfriend. Somehow, I feel like I'd be using my daughter's body to have sex, which in reality I would be. This is getting to weird, let's talk about something else. We stared at each other for a long moment before breaking out in laughter.

I have to tell you about the people at the hospital that is much more interesting. Two hours later we got up from the couch to go outside and play with dogs. When the dogs looked exhausted, we all went inside. Bella went to her bed in the corner and curled up. Max, not having a bed yet, decided Bella would have to share and went over to Bella and stood there. We waited to see what Bella would do. Max stepped into the bed and curled up next to Bella. Bella put her front paw over top of Max. I grabbed my camera and took at least 20 pictures.

Margaret, I began, I am so glad I have someone to talk to about this. Greta, from the hospital, I have to talk to her at least once a day or so until I start seeing the psychiatrist here. Since my donor surgery as I call it, because what else could I call it, I have to have a coping skill. Well, you Margaret are one of them and the other is, I look into the mirror and ask Nicole. Since I know her, and it's her face and voice she kinda tells me what I need to hear. She looked at me and smiled. That sounds perfectly sane. I stared at her then started laughing and couldn't stop laughing. After wiping the tears from my eyes, I finally caught my breath and said, thanks for not letting my grief swallow me up.

Margaret took me by the hand and walked me to the door. I will see you my- wow, ok, I will see you Saturday the day after tomorrow. Now, if you want me to come over tomorrow after work, I can do that. I will be fine, I hugged her. I have appointments to make and shopping to do and a puppy to cuddle, I will see you Saturday. She took the bags from the porch and waved good bye.

I closed the door and leaned up against it. Ok, home I am back and with a new friend who I hope doesn't leave her mark on your floors. Since my husband had died, I had started talking to my house just to hear another human voice. We have two and half months before I go back to the working world. I needed to go food shopping and pickup my mail at the post office. I sat down and made a list and decided I didn't really feel like cooking.

I went to the post office first. When I got to the counter and asked for my mail, the woman looked at me oddly then went to get my mail. She came back with a small box filled with mail. As she put it on the counter, she said, I am very sorry for your loss, how are you doing? I said, thank you I am putting all the pieces back together again, like Humpty-Dumpty I thought. I looked in the box and there are lots of card sized envelopes. I took the box and left. I put it into the back seat and headed for the store across town, I didn't want to run into any one. Shopping took longer in a different store, but I also needed puppy food. I couldn't wait to get home to see how Max and Bella were getting along.

When I got home, the dogs were still sleeping, and didn't even greet me, really, I thought. I put all the groceries away except for the meatloaf tv dinner which I popped into the microwave. I sat at the dining room table and separated all the mail. There were over 100 card shaped envelopes. An idea struck me, I could put the cards on a foam board for the memorial, like a collage. I could print out pictures from the time Nicole was a baby until now.

I cleaned up and decided to wake the dogs. Ok you two, outside with you both, I turned on the outside lights put a bowl of water and a tug-toy on the step. I wanted them to get good and tired and sleep hopefully the whole night through.

I called Greta and told her about my flight, the puppy, and Margaret helping me. She asked me how I was doing now that I was home. I told her that I had picked up my mail and had over a hundred condolence cards. When I unpacked, I realized all the clothes in my closet didn't fit me, I packed them up and Margaret took them to a donation bin. I told her about the rings I had bought. The very weird and uncomfortable conversation with Margaret about me kissing a man or having sex with my daughter's body. I finally stopped talking. Lisa, that is a lot to think about. One thing we have talked about is that you have a new body. You are the mother that created that body. Your daughter is in heaven. You didn't want your daughter to die, nor did you want to die. You made a choice and one I believe any mother would have made. It is your body now. It will take time to fully realize that. If you choose to date a man, it's your mind, it's your body that is in the relationship. She made all seem so sensible. We talked for almost an hour. When I hung up, I was again filled with loneliness.

It was getting late, so I went outside to make sure both dogs had made their deposits into the potty pen. We all trotted upstairs and I changed for bed. Bella who slept with me had no trouble jumping up on the bed. Max however, cried trying to jump up. I took some pictures of her so cute ripping up my bed spread. I picked her up and had to just squeeze her for a moment before putting her next to Bella. It was bad enough Bella sprawled out lengthwise on my bed, now we had company. As I laid down, Max decided to plop on my chest. Ok Max no pee-pee in the bed ok.

In the morning Max licked my face until I woke up. I opened my eyes, smiled and said ok I don't feel wet so let's go out. I carried Max because I wasn't sure she could hold it. I filled the water bowl and put a few more toys outside. Today I should start getting Max on a schedule and try to resume my not so normal life. Greta felt that I was the person I am, and I could go on only after grieving for my daughter. Granted I got to see and hear my daughter's face and voice daily.

I went to the bathroom mirror and stared. Ok, Nicole what do you have to say to your mom? **First let me say the puppy is the cutest ever. Mom, you have to get a grip and don't be all pity party. If you want to date Mom you should, just no weirdos or leftovers, I give you my permission if that's what you need. Also, I really do like those tulip earrings. Make my memorial a happy one, period.** I will do my best baby girl.

I let the dogs in, and we all ate breakfast together. My scrambled eggs today were pretty close to the fluffiest. Well, time to do the email and Facebook updates. I wasn't going to tell anyone that I was home because I didn't want all the calls. I sent the pictures of the puppy to Mr. Dupree. I sent more thanks you and expressed the heart felt comfort I received from them. There were so many of Nicole's classmates, and friends it was a comfort to me having them share their memories. My sorrow was shared by so many, and it felt like less of a weight on my heart. It was noon by the time I finished all the emails and regular mail. I had the packet of papers from Mr. Dupree and the files from the doctors.

They would be another day. I would call to make my appointments with Greta's sister today and also the neurosurgeon. I got my appointment with Gertrude, no surprise in that name, on Monday at one o'clock. That trip would take about 45 minutes. Dr. Light was much closer and only 25 minutes away; for Monday at nine o'clock.

Since it was Friday, my neighbors were at work. Across the street from my house are woods so I have half the number of neighbors. Two of my neighbors were elderly women in their 90's. Another was a couple about to retire in their mid- sixties and the other couple were in their early 20's and worked two jobs, so practically nobody ever saw them. I didn't think any of the neighbors would come running out to greet me, or at least I hoped not. I took the dogs for a quick walk. I looped the other end of the lease around Max and held the lease in the middle. The puppy was so cute, I just wanted to carry her.

I decided to take both dogs with me to the pet store. Max needed a collar and lease, and she looked sad and needed me to cuddle her more. Bella and Max liked the choices I made for treats and toys. Max was too little to walk in the store, I figured I'd better carry her. We left the pet store a couple hundred dollars lighter but at least Max had everything a puppy could want.

On the drive home, I thought about Max. When your life is in great turmoil or sorrow, getting a puppy helps you put your life into perspective. Puppies need water, food, a bed, and contact or cuddles. Life in its simplest form, and the joy of a sleeping puppy who feels safe snuggled up against you. I wonder if Greta told Mr. Dupree that a puppy was a good idea, or if he asked her; if it would be a good idea.

When we got home the dogs played outside with their new toys. It was dinner time. I opened the freezer and got out about six Bitterballens since I had to ration them until Margaret learned how to make them. I let the dogs in and fed them. We were going to do a marathon of tv shows I had missed with chocolate ice-cream and buttered popcorn.

The day went smoothly with Max understanding completely that no pee-pee meant outside. My neighbors saw me walking Max and Bella and gave their condolences. I have to stop by each of the elderly women's homes to show them Max. Since the weather was mild a 46 degrees and sunny, I wore my sunglasses and continued wearing my head scarf daily. Margaret stopped by on Saturday and we spent some time together having lunch and catching a movie. I continued with running both Saturday and Sunday. I had so much more energy and sense of well-being after running.

I called Greta each day and gave her a run down on Max's artistic abilities on holy a la bedspread, pilfer a la pillow, toilet a la bowl. I sent her and Mr. Dupree plenty of pictures. I told her I was looking forward to meeting her sister and asked if she and her were alike. Greta didn't answer at first then she said let's put it this way, if we were side by side most people would not guess we are sisters. Yikes, ok then. I look forward to meeting her on Monday.

Monday morning came soon enough. My first appointment of the day was with Dr. Light. I took the parkway and got there in record time. The building was massive it was almost as wide as it was tall with 15 floors. I found the front door and walked to the front desk. A woman behind the counter asked my name. I gave it to her, and apparently, I was on the list. The third-floor suite 94. I found my way rather easily considering I was so nervous. When I walked in the office; there was a small waiting area with six seats and a tiny window. I went to the window and looked in. The nurse saw me and opened the window, are you Mrs. Goodwin? Yes, I am. Dr. Light will be with you in a few minutes please take a seat. Alrighty then I thought to myself; no sign in, co-pay, fill out these forms please, this is how a doctor's office should be, they just know you. I held the file YU which has all kinds of brain images and a few taken during the surgery. The brain image with an X was Nicole's. I couldn't read all the medical terms. I closed the file and then closed my eyes. It was an amazing surgery success. The emotional ramifications I was still on the fence. I had daily talks with a psychiatrist, two coping go-to-strategies, and a puppy. I could do this.

After a few minutes the inner office door opened. He looked just like his cousin Dr. Lambs. What are the chances. I stood up to shake his hand. Hello Mrs. Goodwin, I am Dr. Light, please come with me to my office he said with an accent. I followed him through long 3 long corridors. He opened the door to his enormous office which had three giant screens and a large table enough to fit 20 people. His desk was in a corner of the room with an arm chair next to it. Please do sit down. When I sat; I handed him the file. He check the name and I saw him smile.

I have read up on all the tests that you were given just before leaving the hospital. It's not quite a month since your surgery. How are you feeling, any headaches, problems coordinating hand, leg, or eye movements? I have only had a few small headaches when I am thinking too much about everything. Ahh, yes, maybe you were upset? Yes, I was. The increase of blood flow and stress can cause this, and it is normal. As far as movement I am fine, I am actually running almost every day, which is something I never did before. It was your daughter, Nicole, she was a runner yes? She was. Dr. Light looked at me for a moment then asked, may I check your scars? I took off the head scarf. It is healing very quickly and looks like you won't have much of a scar, the hair is growing around and on the closure. What I would like to do today is a fluids panel test. Have you had any bowel problems? No, I haven't. Please let me know if you do. I will be taking blood samples and urine samples. He turned on his computer and created labels for the tests then printed them out. He opened one of his drawers and pulled out six glass vials and put the labels on. I looked at him, and said, doesn't the nurse usually do this? In a hospital situation yes, the nurse would. Here we do research and it's important that the researcher know and do as much of the testing themselves. Also, this type of research is highly sensitive, and privacy is paramount as I am sure Dr. Lambs and Dr. Vinke explained to you. Yes, of course I said, do you like my file name? He smiled and said yes, Dr. Lambs said you had a sense of humor.

After drawing almost all the blood in my body, he went to a panel on the wall which was really a refrigerator and took out an orange juice. Here, drink this then I will need the urine samples. He asked me to fill the bathroom urine bowl if possible, nope not possible.

When I was finished. He asked me to sit down. We will run many different types of tests. We are interested in seeing how your brain being the older and what we call in families the originator reacts to its replication system meaning your daughter's body. We will check everything from hair and nail growth after 6 months. After a surgery the body goes into over drive and shock.

Doctor does that mean, the body and brain could reject each other? No, not at all, if that were the case, they would have known within 72 hours. We are looking for how your brain reads and responses to the body's systems. Dr. Vinke's test results all came back in the normal range. Do you have any concerns or questions? Should I have any questions doctor? How are you feeling mentally and are you sleeping ok? I am sleeping ok, mentally it's weird, but I have Greta and Margaret who are helping me grieve and make sense of my life. Good, I am glad you have support. Next week after we run these samples, I will contact Dr. Lambs and Dr. Vinke and we will see where we go from there.

I left his office and had plenty of time to make it to make it to my appointment with Gertrude. I got there a little early. When I walked into the reception area and gave my name, I expected to fill out papers and such, but no paper work. I wished every office was like this. The room had about four others waiting, and I found a seat. This office had quite a few doctors in it. I leaned over to select a magazine when the receptionist called my name. I got up and walked to the door and she buzzed me in. Straight ahead. I walked to the door straight ahead and knocked. "Come in" a gruff voice called. Was this a man-sister, because this did not sound like Greta, or what I thought her sister would sound like. I opened the door and found, yikes, a big husky tall woman was standing by her desk. Now this I thought should be interesting. I slowly walked up to her with my hand extended. Gertrude's hand completely engulfed mine with a stern shake.

"Please sit" she said in that mannish voice. I sat down feeling awkward. Gertrude's appearance was so different than Greta's, she was, or could be a man. Her eyes though, were just like Greta's. I didn't know if I could get used to her voice. Mrs. Goodwin, I have read your file and have talked at length with Greta. I have some forms to give you which you will take home and fill out daily. They take only about 5 minutes to complete. It's very important that you fill it out very carefully and thoughtfully each and every time. Do you understand what I mean by carefully and thoughtfully?

Sure, I should take the time to think truthfully about each and every answer. Yes, that is correct, said Gertrude in a firm voice. She handed me a small booklet. The booklet had her strong handwriting on the cover with the dates to be completed and under the name it had in capital letters YU, I laughed to myself, afraid to laugh a loud. I placed it carefully in my purse then looked up at her.

Do you have any concerns you would like to address or questions? I felt like I was being interviewed and wanted to run. Well, no not right now, I have a note pad that I write down things I think so I don't forget and call or email Greta or Dr. Vinke.

Gertrude's lips pursed and she said, I like that you write down questions and concerns please continue with this practice. You can bring your note pad to our next session in a week and we will discuss them. Today, let's talk about what you think about your future in the next few months and expand it to this year.

Well, I wanted to have my daughter's memorial around February 9th. I am going back to work April 1st.   I was planning, before this accident to retire in a couple of years, but now I am starting to rethink that.

Good, you have been planning short term and the future. Why are you rethinking about your retirement?

I looked at Gertrude, which was hard to do, after knowing her sister. I want to travel with my dogs now. I want to have them service trained so I can bring them with me everywhere. I always had a dream of raising service dogs.

Sounds like you know where you are headed. That is very good. Now, tell me how are you doing now do you have trouble sleeping, remembering things, completing simple daily tasks?

No, I pretty much write most things down and well I am a list maker. I don't always complete everything on my list, and it's in no particular order either; I do try to be realistic.

Tell me about your go-to- coping strategies, Gertrude asked with a lift of her lips. I guessed that was the closest she came to a smile.

I have my long -time trusted friend, Margaret who knows me and all that has happened. She has always been my reliable reasonable consciousness. I have known her since we were born our mothers put us in the play pen together. Being able to talk to her has been; almost I would say a relief.

My other coping strategy is talking to my daughter in the mirror. When I miss her, I look in the mirror and see and hear her voice. She talks to me, rather I talk, she speaks. I folded my hands in my lap and looked down at them. The silence grew so loud I could hear it ringing in my ears.

Finally, Gertrude spoke in a low gruff tone. How do you feel when you look into the mirror and see your daughter?

That's a question I don't know how to answer I thought. Well, when I look into the mirror; I sometimes think I am going to see my face, but I always smile when I see her there looking back at me. I love my daughter more than anything on this earth. She is part of me and gave me hope of true love the day she was born. The true bond of love in mother and daughter, love that breathes joy, happiness, and unconditional acceptance. She speaks to me with her heart.

We sat in silence contemplating what was said. After a few minutes, Gertrude got up and walked over to me and sat in the chair next to me. She stared at me until I met her gaze. You are a very loving and brave woman whose journey has just begun. I believe not many people could do what you did and feel the essence of life between you both. If you have any concerns, you may call me at any time. I will see you next Monday with your booklet filled out.

Thank you, I said, and left.

I felt odd and yet new, like I found out something about myself that I didn't know. Gertrude was definitely going to be interesting. When I got into my car, I pulled out the booklet, now interested in what I had to fill out each week. When I opened it, I was surprise to find it was like the tests I give in school. There were questions with bubble rating choices, from 0 to 5. The directions were; Did you at any time during this day only …. then the list of feelings and actions like coordination, confusion, remembering. I hope I don't start dreaming about these questions. I know what Nicole would do, she would put 0 then a 5, then 0 then another 5 down the whole list. I laughed out loud, and someone walking by stared at me. This kind of office, I am sure some people laugh inside and outside, hum maybe too much.

I needed to get home and let Max out; this would be the longest time she hasn't gone out. I hoped that Bella could convince her to hold it. Bella was a good teacher. I let both dogs out and gave them water and toys.

I called Margaret and told her about my visits with the different doctors and my booklet. We laughed when I told her how different Gertrude was than Greta. Margaret asked if I needed her to come over tonight. No, I am good. Margaret was a teacher also and had a husband two cats, a dog, a rabbit and an indoor garden room with herbs and plants. She was also a very good cook. She said she had perfected the Bitterballens and would bring them over Saturday.

The air was brisk, but the temperature was 42 degrees so, I took the dogs with me for a run. It was easier to teach Max on a lease because she had to concentrate on keeping up with us. I had a water bottle attached to my belt and gave both dogs all my water. They would sleep good tonight.

I didn't feel like cooking, so a TV dinner was popped into the microwave, then I turned on the TV, you have to watch TV with a TV dinner. When Nicole had left for college, my husband and I took to watching the evening news while we ate our dinner in the living room. When he died last year, I just kept up the tradition.

After dinner cleanup, which wasn't much, I checked the freezer, I was out of dinners, and more importantly I was out of ice-cream. I would have to go to the store. I put on my head scarf, which I was really getting used to, doesn't matter what kind of

• • •
117

hair day you are having. My hair was still sticking up and not yet able to lay flat. I grabbed my keys and decided I would just go around the corner; as there shouldn't be that many people, I know shopping at 7pm.

Well, I was wrong. Just as I pulled out the cart from the stack, I saw Cole. I don't know how he recognized me, but he did. Cole was a teacher and good friend. My daughter used to babysit his little girl. His wife and daughter had died four years ago in an auto accident. He went to grief group counseling and for about nine months he dragged me with him after my husband died. He was a good person and friend.

Hi Cole, this was going to be awkward. He came up and just wrapped his arms around me. I almost started crying and was blinking my eyes rapidly. When he pulled away, he his eyes were as wet as mine. He started to talk but had to clear his throat first. I am so very sorry for all that you have been through. I looked at him for a moment trying to speak. I know Cole, I just got home a few days ago, but I didn't want anyone to know, I just needed some time first. I am not coming back to work until April.

He looked at me and said let's go shopping and we can talk. He was so easy going and also knew how to put people at ease. It took us over an hour to shop and talk our way around every aisle. While we were still in the checkout line, Cole asked, the grief group is tomorrow would you like me to pick you up? I wasn't sure I wanted to go, I knew most of the people, what else was I doing. Yes, Cole that would be good for me. Ok then, I will pick you up tomorrow.

I got home and let the dogs out then put away all my groceries. I bought a lot of healthy foods, just because Cole was with me. Normally I would stock up on TV dinners, ice-cream, chips and chocolate. Certain potato chips taste really good with chocolate. Cooking for one is; well boring, because you know you will be having the same thing the next day or day after. I showered and got into another pair of new pjs. I let the dogs in, and they ran upstairs to my bed, so I figured it was bed time.

Little Max was crying trying to get up on the bed. Bella jumped down grabbed Max by the neck and hoisted her up. At first, I almost screamed thinking Bella was annoyed, and I can't think about what I thought was going to happen. I picked up my phone and took some pictures. These two were friends. I pushed them over some so I could get into bed. Max decided to plop onto of my chest. I took her two front paws and played peek-a-boo with her. Then I had an idea, I reached over for my phone and turned on the camera and leaned it against my chin. I used

Max's two front paws to wave while I talked in a baby voice. When I opened my mouth wide so would Max, so the video came out so cute. Bella was not impressed and was fast asleep snoring.

The next morning, we all went for a run and came home for breakfast. The canines got their kibble, and for me; almost the fluffiest eggs ever. After I cleaned up, I sat down to email Greta and Mr. Dupree, of course I sent them the video of Max talking. I watched the video like 10 times. I wasn't sure what to write to Greta about her sister. So, I used her comment, yep I would have never guessed you were sisters. I also told her I had run into an old friend and that tonight we were going to Grief Counseling Group which I had gone to before when my husband died.

After I checked and sent emails and updates on Facebook I sat thinking about yesterday. I wondered how Cole recognized me in just the parking lot lights. He knew my car I guessed; how many people own an orange Lexus. He didn't say anything about the head scarf, but would anyone? My neighbors didn't seem to think that I was Nicole trying to be her mom. I supposed the make-up, my using a higher voice tone with my personality made them see me. Would this work with kids? My students were 10 years old and not easily tricked. By the time April comes around it will be three and a half months since they have seen me. I would still be wearing the head scarf, since hair only grows about a half an inch each month. My hair would be less than 2 inches when I returned to school. I could dye it red in March. I had to stop thinking too hard. One thing at a time focus.

I wanted to bring something for the group for snack, so I made vanilla chip cupcakes with light blue icing and edible snowflakes. Most of the time I would make cupcakes or brownies with sweet cream frosting. They were the only things I knew how to make without doing them over cooked or under cooked. I would call them my specialty, but since it's the only thing I could make it didn't seem right. I packed them up in a cupcake case and left them by the door.

Well, I had the rest of the day. The elephant in the room was not budging at all. I had put up the Christmas tree in the corner. I didn't put any other decorations up inside or outside; as I didn't know how Nicole would react. There were no presents as I had given them out before we left for our trip. Nicole and I agreed we would get each other presents while in Amsterdam. I went to the basement and brought up all the boxes to pack the tree and the ornaments. It took about three hours to pack up and put everything back in the basement.

I let the dogs out and decided it was time for a nap. How was I going to fill my time up before I went back to school? I got out the booklet and decided that today would be day 1. It took me 30 minutes to really read, think about the ratings, then fill it out. I made a quick dinner for myself and fed the dogs. I wanted to take Max for another run to get her tired out, if that was possible. We went for a long run and walk and when we got home Bella flopped on the rug. I showered and changed into what I would wear that night. I found a large bag and put a soft towel in it and placed it next to the door with my keys and some water.

At exactly 6:45 Cole pulled up, so I filled my bag, grabbed my cupcakes and was out the door. Hi Cole, this feels like Déjà vu. Yes, it does. I know a lot of regulars will …hum that doesn't sound right to say. I know what you mean, I miss seeing them too. Thank you, Cole, for being there for me and dragging me out. Cole gave me a run down on all the regulars in the Grief Counseling Group and told me about the new members.   There are some regulars like Cole, who have been going for years and they have formed a strong bond with the other long- time members of the group. After my husband died, Cole dragged to me meetings monthly. The group meets once a month except for November, December, and January they meet twice a month to help members during the holidays. Now, Lisa we have a grumpy new member and well, he doesn't like people to much, so please don't try to get him to talk. Yes sir; who is the grumpy member? His name is Sam and as soon as you see him you will know that he is grumpy, yea, he looks grumpy.

When we went in; I was filled with happiness seeing so many regulars welcoming me and really heartfelt sorrow for my loss. I didn't feel lonely. These people understood and cared for each other and me. Ouch, grumpy ahead. You could not miss grumpy, he was old and had one of the scariest old people faces I had ever seen, like the kind you see in haunted houses during Halloween. He was sitting by himself looking down at his hands. I felt so sorry for him. I sat next to him and put my bag in between our chairs. Everyone else started to find seats. Cole sat on the other side of me. Lula who ran the meetings started with welcoming me back. I felt shaky and wasn't sure I could talk. I thanked everyone, then told them about my loss of my daughter, and how we went on a trip to get away since my husband had died a year ago, I didn't know I would be coming home alone. There were tears and coughs, and I did my best to blink away my tears. I told them how good I felt being there with all of them and that I had really missed them. I then sat silently waiting for someone else to speak. Lula took the cue and asked someone else to talk about how they got through the holidays. I looked down at my bag which was open. Sam looked at me then at my bag. He said in a low rough tone, which made me think of Gertrude, is that real or stuffed?

I smiled and said real, I picked up the sleepy Max and put him into Sam's lap. Max woke and licked Sam's hand and put her head down on his hand. He started to stroke Max and she went back to sleep. I turned to look at Cole, who had seen the whole exchange. How did you get a sleeping puppy in here? I whisper to him, well I took her for a two-mile run before we came, so I knew she would sleep for a few hours. It's called plan ahead. No one had noticed that Sam had a sleeping puppy on his lap. I wondered if anyone talked to him after group, or even looked at him. He looks really mean and grumpy which I guess would put off most people.

A few more people had talked about how they coped with the holidays. Max woke and started licking and wagging her tail in Sam's lap. Now, someone noticed and there was a "How cute" and "A puppy". When I looked at Sam he was, I guess for him, smiling. By now everyone was staring at him. I didn't want him to feel uncomfortable, so I said; this is one of my coping strategies and I can tell you it really works. I talked about how I had gotten her, and how it helped even Bella. I even suggested everyone should get a puppy. Some people got up to pet Max and commented to Sam he should get a puppy as it was obvious, he was good with puppies. Now everyone wanted a chance to hold Max and Sam would lift her to the next waiting pair of hands. Someone asked what kind of dog Max was. I explained that she was a Czechoslovakia shepherd - wolf dog, mostly used in police work and bred in Czechoslovakia. I didn't know if we would even get out of there. The "so called meeting" ran well into overtime with Max being the star of the show. While Sam handed over Max to different people, well everybody, Cole and I decided it was a good time to see what snacks everybody brought, and we got first dibs.

We found a land mine of boxes of chocolates and cookies which had never been opened. I looked at Cole and said, they must have gotten these over the holidays and never opened them. Cole said, it's easier to eat with people, and food somehow tastes better when eaten with others. I laughed and Cole looked surprised. I am sorry, I am not laughing at you. It's well; to be honest, when we were shopping together last- night I bought all kinds of healthy foods, because I didn't want you to think I was a lazy slob just getting TV dinners. He stared at me for a long moment, which made me feel uneasy, then chuckled. Well let me tell you Lisa, do you remember I told you I was taking cooking classes after school? Yes, I do, something Happy Health?

Hey, you remembered. Well, I can honestly say I am a good cook and can make something out of anything you give me. So, if you want to get rid of that healthy food, I can come over and cook for you. Oh yes please do get rid of my healthy food. Can you start tomorrow? Sure, after school I will stop over and cook you a meal better than any meal you have ever had. Sounds like a plan. When it was time to leave because it was almost an hour after our usual time, Sam handed over Max, and said you ought to bring her next time she was a big hit. Sure, thing Sam see you in couple weeks.

On our way home Cole laughed and said, well I guess you talked to grumpy Sam in your own way. Yea, like who doesn't love a puppy. I think I even saw his teeth in what could be described as a smile. Sam lost his wife of 45 years and hasn't been out of the house in over a year and half. He wouldn't leave the house and move in with one of his children, and really wouldn't go out for anything, he was afraid they would put him into a nursing home or something. His children were so concerned they called doctor, and the office of aging in hopes of getting him emotional help. The doctor, who is a friend of mine suggested he come here. The office of aging convinced him he had the right to stay in his home. So; he has been coming for about 3 months now. That is so sad Cole, he needs a friend, or maybe a puppy. It would force him to get out a couple times a day and he would have to get puppy food, so he would have to go to the store.

I don't know that a puppy solves all the problems, I just think you want everyone to have a puppy. Hey, they are a comfort. When we pulled up to my house, Cole said, ok I will see you about four o'clock. You are serious aren't you! We gotta get that healthy food out of your house. I laughed and said see you tomorrow then.

Bella was happy to see me, and I gave her lots of hugs, then I let both dogs out. I was so proud of Max; not one accident yet or that I knew of anyway. I got ready for bed and let the dogs in. It's funny how Bella knows its bed time, maybe she knows when she sees my pjs. This time when we went upstairs, Bella took Max by the neck and put her on the bed. It was so sweet watching Bella get on the bed and nudge Max over to get enough room so she could stretch out. Max plopped down on my chest, I hope she didn't think she could do this when she got bigger. I played pee-a-boo with her front paws and couldn't stop laughing. We cuddled until morning came.

The next morning, I came even closer to the fluffiest eggs ever. The dogs spent the morning outside running around in the snow that started falling. I watched them from the window. Max was making

Bella act like a puppy. I started thinking about grumpy Sam and was sure he needed a friend. I went to my computer and started reading emails and Facebook. I had to start telling people I was home, but I wanted to wait until the memorial for Nicole which would be in a few weeks.

Instead I looked on-line for small dog adoption. After almost two and half hours I found one. It was a mixed toy-Poodle and Bichon Frise and would be available in a week for adoption. I contacted the phone listed and discussed the details about picking up the puppy in two weeks.

With that done, I had to call the dogs to come in. They ate and I cleaned the kitchen up, since Cole was coming over, I didn't want him to see the kitchen out of order. I felt like I had to overdo it because I was home all day. I put out the cutting board and put some knives out along with the basic spices, salt, pepper and oil.

With that done, I took the dogs out for a run. I was really enjoying running or jogging or whatever they called it these days. Nicole would make fun of me always using terms that were so outdated. I could see and feel the appeal. It's almost a high you get from running and you feel so good afterwards. Plus, Max needed it as I didn't want her to get bored and find the house a playground as she already did with my pillow.

When we got back the dogs dropped onto the floor to nap. I got showered and ready since Cole would be here in about an hour.

I got out the photo boxes of pictures of Nicole and put them on my desk. I had a few weeks to make a collage of pictures. There still was the matter of getting her stuff from her dorm room. Nicole had finished up her classes and was due to graduate in May with a master's in science. Her life was just starting. What if I took over her life? I would have to work for the next 35 some years. I didn't know anything about her master's degree. Could I pull it off, and wouldn't it be easier to try to be her than me? As I thought about it, I came to one conclusion, I didn't want to work for the next 35 years, so no I wouldn't try to be her. I went into the bathroom mirror, tried to smirk, still no success there. **Mom, you are doing ok, don't make it more work than it should be. Take a breath mint before Cole gets here, I like him Mom. He is a great guy even if he is a younger man. You also need to make more videos of Max playing peek-a-boo and post them, they will go viral.** Ok baby girl, thanks and I will do my best.

I started thinking about Cole, he was seven years younger than me, now 15 years older than my body. Well if that isn't weird Sci-Fi stuff, I don't know what is. Cole was to me a trusting dependable co-worker and friend, whom Nicole babysat for. He was very easy on the eyes and had a tough-guy appearance about him. I didn't think our relationship was more than that, but could it be? I hadn't even thought about dating my husband died. There had been in the last couple of months a few men who have asked me out to dinner, but I just flatly said no. Geeze-Louise for crying in a bucket, Cole is just coming over to get rid of my healthy food and tomorrow while he is at work, I can go buy some TV dinners.

I sat down and filled out my booklet like a good little girl. It took me over 10 minutes to fill out. Then, I got onto the computer and emailed Greta. I missed her so much. I wondered if I could get her to do video call. I sent her and Mr. Dupree more pics of Max and Bella and told them how Max was the star of the show at Grief Counseling Group. I also emailed the doctors and told them about my visit to the research facility. A knock on the door startled me and I shut down the computer and went to greet Cole.

Hi, Lisa I am here to relieve you of healthy foods that may contaminate your home. Where are the pups? Oh, we went for a run and well they are pretty much sacked out in the living room. Cole looked at me and said, I didn't know you ran, I know Nicole did; sometimes her and I would run the path at the park together when she was at home. I used to tell her she shouldn't run alone, so she said I would be her body guard. Yea, well, I just kinda started because Max is needing an outlet to help exert energy, I said in a voice that I hoped sounded believable. This is going to be harder than I thought. Cole shook his head and laughed, hey let's take the pups to the path this Saturday morning about 7:30; you in? Sure, I can train you how to run with a dog which isn't that easy, it may take a few lessons. We walked into the kitchen and Cole smiled, you hungry or what, I see you have the supplies out. Well, I said, sort of-kinda; yea! Ok, then I will cook you can set the table and pour drinks. I have some red wine; I will crack it open now for us.

Over dinner which was so much better than I could have ever done, Cole told me about my substitute teacher and how my students were fairing without me. He talked about the gossip and things going on at school so I would be up to date on everybody and everything.

After dinner we put the dishes in the dishwasher, and Cole said, hey I have something for you I will be right back. Ok, I said finishing up the clean-up. He went out to his car and retrieved a large brown envelope and handed it to me. I dried my hands and opened it. There were lots and lots of construction paper folded cards the students from school had made for me. This is so heartwarming I said with wet eyes. Cole gave my hand a little squeeze and said they miss you and care about you. There are notes and letters from the teachers and workers from the school as well.

It gave me an idea to use these also for the memorial. I told Cole about my plans to have the memorial and all the cards I received on display. He said he had lots of extra-large sized foam poster board I could use for the display and that he had little metal stands for them. This will take time, but hey, I have lots of time now, so it should keep me busy for the next few weeks. Well, I can bring the boards over tomorrow after work. That would be great, thank you Cole. We sat and read some of the cards, commenting on spelling and their artist abilities with gel pens and glitter.

I got up to get more wine for us both, I opened the refrigerator and screamed COLE, oh my gosh, come look. He jerked up concerned and stood beside me looking into the refrigerator, WHAT! There is still healthy food in here, it might contaminate my home! He stared at me in disbelief, then broke out in hysterical laughter. Ok, ok, I will stop over tomorrow with the boards and get this healthy food out. Ok then, I will make dessert tomorrow.

I let the dogs out after Cole left. I started thinking about the comment I had made about running. Such a little thing. Would Cole figure out my secret? My secret sounded like a movie or book. I knew in my heart I could trust Cole. I felt somehow awkward about myself. Hey, it's me in my daughter's body, creepy right. I had to keep reminding myself what Greta had told me. Mind, body and soul are one and that one is me. I had to focus on one thing at a time. Like, tomorrow Cole would bring the boards and make dinner, which means I had to make dessert. I am not a cook, but I am a great shopper and know a great bakery who makes blueberry pies. Yea, oh yea I am slipping the pie into one of my pie dishes, I am shameless. I got out the pie dish I would use tomorrow. I put all the cards back into the envelope and put onto my desk with the others and let the dogs in.

We all ran upstairs for bed, Bella helping Max get up on the bed. This time I was ready with my phone camera. When we all got settled in, Max wanted to play peek-a-boo, well she plopped down on my chest, so I figured that was her way of saying let's play. This video was the cutest ever, Max laughing in her little girl voice saying, "What day do chickens hate most? Fry-day". Then we all snuggled in and slept peacefully.

Max woke me up, and I quickly got up and carried her outside with Bella. I was tired, or maybe it was from the wine last night. I poured some cereal in a bowl and stood watching the pups play outside. I called the bakery to make sure they had a blueberry pie and that I would be over later to pick it up. I sat down at my laptop and watched the video I had made last night and uploaded it. Nicole would have loved Max. I also sent it to Greta and Mr. Dupree.

I picked up the pie and some vanilla ice-cream to go with it. I took the dogs for a long run, which Max had to be carried part of the way home. Bella was enjoying the running. We were all tired and decided to take a nap when we got home. I changed into my pjs and lay on the bed which Bella and Max were already snoring on. Bella woke up and rearranged herself next to me and lay her head on my stomach looking at me. Bella, I whispered as I gently stroked her. As she stared at me, I knew that she knew it was me. She never snuggled with anyone else like this but me.

After a few hours, I woke up to sleeping dogs everywhere. Maybe I should get king size bed. I really needed more room to sleep and Max wasn't going to get smaller. I dressed and went downstairs to set up the kitchen and set the table. Cole would be here in less than an hour, so I went into in a tiny spare room that had my desk and cleared my crafting table. I would need room to make these posters for the memorial.

A loud knock on the door woke the dogs and had them running to the door. I went to the door to find giant posters with arms wrapped around them. I quickly opened the door to help Cole. Here take these I have more in the car. I turned them sideways so they would fit through the door and brought them into the room and lay them onto the crafting table. I went back to the front door as Cole was coming up with more, here take these and I will get the metal holders for them. I let the dogs out and Cole gave me a bag with the metal holders. Kitchen is calling Cole, Cole. He laughed; the master chef is here to save the day. As he started dinner and I was sorting through the poster boards, he yelled, I love blueberry pie. Great I said, hoping I put enough trash over the box it came in. I went into the kitchen and started cleaning up the cut off ends of veggies to toss more in the trash compactor, let me help. Feeling my secret was safe for now, I poured some wine for us.

Over dinner I told Cole about my plan to give Sam a puppy that needed adoption. He thought it was a great idea, but asked, what if he doesn't want a puppy. I didn't think of that, because I am sure he will love the puppy, and if not, you can take the puppy home. What did you say? I said you could take the puppy home. No, I just moved and can't take care of a dog. What do you mean you moved? Well, the house was too big for me and someone gave me an offer I couldn't refuse, so as of January 1st I live at the old wind mill place by the river. I love that place, it's next to the park and a river runs through the yard. Yep, that's the place. I left most of my furniture at the house, because I wanted to start fresh. I just finished the painting, then sanding and staining all the floors, which is easy since I have no furniture. It looks brand new inside. The outside was just sided with cedar and a new roof and decking. I am looking forward to spring, since Sally who does the landscaping in the park, blended the landscaping into the yard so it looks like part of the park. I have the windmill for some power to. It's only two bedrooms and small but it's all I need. Ok Cole, old buddy of mine, I want to come sit on your porch in the spring, I will bring coffee and coffee cake. That place is so quaint, I just love that place. Could we switch houses? No, I am falling in love with the place.

Why don't I make dinner for us at my place tomorrow? You can come over about 5:00. I don't have a table and chairs yet. I will bring my folding chair. I can't wait to see what you have done. Over blueberry pie and ice-cream Cole describe how he started with the kitchen, because he is still taking night classes in cooking-part two. So, basically the kitchen is the only room done. I am lacking in the décor department and maybe you can give me some ideas. You called the right person. I love to decorate. I can't wait to see it tomorrow.

I turned on the dishwasher after Cole left, and I filled out my little booklet. Since it was only Thursday, I had a few more days before I had to go back to see Gertrude, and Dr. Light on Monday. I was excited to about seeing Cole's new home. I should bring a dessert, wine, and a housewarming gift, and better not forget a folding chair so I can sit down. I made a list, let the dogs in. I went to my crafting table and started on the boards for the memorial. I started with putting all the cards I had received in the mail. Glue dots were amazing; every home should have them. Next, I did a few boards with the cute cards students had made for me and Nicole. I started on the photos starting with her being a baby up to college. It was really late, and I was dog-tired.

It was becoming a routine with the dogs. I pushed my way into bed with my phone. Max jumped onto my chest and lay flat. After a minute of peek-a-boo, Max's little voice, "What do you call a cold dog; a chilidog!" I posted the video and sent it to Greta and Mr. Dupree. I hope they didn't think I was corny. I checked the video from the previous night, it already had over 391 hits. Ok, I thought; people need to get out more. We snuggled and slept like babies.

We got up early, had a run, breakfast, and a short nap. I went out in search of a housewarming gift. I wore my winter hat, and since the sun was out my sunglasses. I had to go to the mall and really did not want to run into anyone I knew, especially any of my students' parents. I went into a Kitchen Korner and found a stone knife block with some very impressive knives. The cost was also very impressive. Geeze, you don't buy a house every day, and Cole's cooking was worth it. I bought them and went into the Engravers Edge. I asked them to put Cole's Kitchen on each of the knives. Since I had to wait, I decided to grab a bit to eat. I went to the food court and got a chilidog with onions and fries. While I sat there, I scanned over the tables to see the people eating. I saw two young girls. One of them was a friend of Nicole's she had known since kindergarten. I started getting nervous, would she recognize me? I put my sunglasses back on feeling like a total dork. Like who eats a hotdog in mall wearing sunglasses! I quickly dumped my trash and went back to the store to wait for the knives. Once they were done, I left the mall and stopped by the bakery to pick up some sticky buns.

Once I was home, I put the folding chair in my car, the wine, and the sticky buns. I did my little booklet and had to change a few choices. I got dressed and headed over to Cole's new home. His house was really close and only took 4 minutes.

The house was small but so very charming. It had a wraparound porch and at one corner a large curved bay window. The door was half leaded glass and lights from within shone out. The door also had side lights on each side of the door. Pretty fancy for a small home. I put the chair down and knocked on the door. After a few minutes he opened the door and took the wine and chair and said, "Welcome to my castle!" The house was totally empty, the floors gleamed of blonde wood. The walls were satin white. This is a beautiful landscape waiting to be painted, I said turning all around to see it all. Come into the kitchen it's the only room done. The kitchen was picture perfect like from out of a magazine. Oh my, this is really impressive, I love your kitchen, your stove, your refrigerator, your dishwasher, your cabinets, your counter. This is so beautiful if I haven't used that word before. Cole, this is wow and I have the perfect housewarming gift for you. I handed him the bag and said, open it now. He placed the bag on the counter and unwrapped the block, it matched perfectly. Then he started unwrapping the knives and saw the engraving and turned to face me. He just flung his arms around me and said thank you this is so kind, I love it and will think of you every time I cut. As long as it's not people. We laughed. He set up my chair next to his at the end of the counter. Sorry no table. Dinner is ready.

After we ate the sticky buns with coffee, he showed me the rest of the house. His bedroom only had a lounge chair in it with a suitcase full of clothes. Are you kidding me, you have no bed? Not yet, I can't decide. You need to get a king size. What are these knobs on the wall? Oh, they are drawers for clothes and storage, all the rooms have them. That is so cool. Ok, look Cole, Sunday we are going furniture shopping. Well, the house is ready to be filled and you do have good taste, so I am happy it's going to be you helping me. Look mister, you did mighty fine in the kitchen yourself.

He started laughing more to himself. What! I asked getting annoyed because I wasn't in on the joke. Let's sit down first, we sat, and he looked at me and said; please don't take this the wrong way or get offended. Cole, we have known each other way to long for that. Just please don't be upset. Now you have to tell me, or I will use a Cole's Kitchen knife on you. Ok, well years ago Ann, my wife, and I talked about if one or the other died we would want the other to remarry and go on. We said we had to approve of each other's choice, or we couldn't remarry. So, who did Ann choose? She choose Dave our vice-principal at school. Good choice that was a smart choice I said. And now who did you pick? I picked you. Me? Yea, even Ann agreed. I know it's weird, it was just the thought of you picking out the furniture for the house reminded me of it. Now I am feeling awkward, what to say, what to do. Ok I say, well I never thought about that kind of thing, but I do feel honored that you chose me and glad that Ann approved. So, who wants a coffee to go, me? He laughed; I hope you don't feel strange. No Cole, I don't but I do need to go since you are dragging me out on the path at the park for running at 7:30 tomorrow, which I now have learned you live right next to. Ok, coffee to go, and tomorrow on my porch 7:30!

When I got home, I let the dogs out and called Margaret right away. I told her everything that Cole had said. Well it's about time she said in an exasperated tone. Really, I say. Has Cole kissed you yet? No, he hasn't, and I really don't know what to do. If I was in my old body, I would be going on a crash diet and be at the gym for 6 to 8 hours a day. In my; yes, I said my new body, I feel more body approval, like it's 15 years younger than him, my old body was 7 years older than him. I am guessing that for Cole, body doesn't matter if he thinks he is getting an older model. You should feel good about yourself, you cougar.

I just don't know. Margaret said, look would you go for it if you were in your old body. Yes, I would. Just because you have a new body your mind is still the same. What was it you said one body and mind? Well maybe I am stressing out for nothing, it's not like he kissed me or wants to date me, I mean, he didn't say that. Lisa, when a man tells you that his go-to girl is you, he wants you, you wild little cougar. Stop calling me cougar, you are crazy. She made a roaring sound and laughed. Whatever, Margaret I will see you tomorrow at 11:00 at our usual place and hung up. I wanted to email Greta, but we had already crossed that bridge. I know she is right, but I just felt weird. I went to stand in front of the mirror door and looked at myself. Well kid, what do you think of your mom. **Mom, you need to go for it. Cole is really cool, and he can cook way better than you can. He is a great man, he is different than dad, and Cole has a goodness you don't often find. I am proud of you mom; he is a great choice. Quit your stressing and cuddle that cute little Max and check the video seen count. I love you mom.** I love you too kid.

I was so tired and knowing I had to get up early made me more tired. I checked the video count, good grief over 521. The pups were already sleeping so I curled up to Bella and put Max next to my chin and we all slept.

None of us were happy campers to wake up at 7:00 am. I tried to sound excited like this would be fun. Yea right, the dogs just ignored me. So, I got up and dressed and made a quick cup of coffee. I got out the wooden spoon and banged it on a pot yelling treats - treats! Now they came running. I opened the door to let them both out, and when they came running back inside, I gave them both a milk-bone treat. I hooked on their leases' and off we went to Cole's new house.

He was standing on the porch waiting for us. Ok what will your poison be, a poodle or wolf? I will take the poodle, no wait, I will take the wolf, Max will help me look more manly. Ok wolf it is. Bella was so excited she danced in a circle. Max tried to copy her but just got tangled up in her lease. One loop or two I asked. Let's do two, then some hot coco. Sounds good to me!

We couldn't talk as I was keeping a steady running pace, and Cole was just one step behind. I chuckled to myself, thinking in a sing-song voice I am younger than you are. I was glad we didn't talk as I was still processing his words from last night. When we did our second loop we then sat down on the steps of his porch. The dogs had enough as well.

Ok, let's go in I have two bowls of water set up for them. Oh, thank you, that is so thoughtful Cole. We went in and I could see he even had the cups for coco ready as well. I just need to microwave them. The dogs drank and we sat. Do you have any.... Yes, I have marshmallows he said before I could finish my sentence. Alrighty then. Cole handed me a cup with three large marshmallows floating on top. We drank in silence watching the dogs.

When we finished the coco, I handed him my cup, he put them in the dishwasher. He looked at me and I squinted my eyes and said, woodsie, eclectic, or nautical style for your furniture. Uh-oh; I have no clue that's why I need your help. Well, we will do all three then. Nautical for the bathroom, woodsie for the dining room and eclectic for the living room.

Lisa, what exactly do you mean by eclectic? Well, we need at least three different colors, and different textured fabrics and designs that blend well. It will be great you will love it. Ok, what do you mean by woodsie? That means we will find a color that matches your kitchen cabinets with a table and bench chair combo and table settings in the brown color family. So, start looking on-line today. What time do you want to go tomorrow? It's Sunday, so most stores open at noon. Sounds good to me. I got up and called the dogs and headed for the door. I have to meet Margaret in another hour. Cole went past me to open the door. I stopped in front of him. I paused thinking yea he really is good looking. I said, I didn't thank you for dropping off the poster boards. It really helps knowing someone cares. My eyes started getting moist and he smiled. You did a lot for me a few years back, and I don't think I ever thanked you. This is my thank you to you. See you tomorrow.

I got home in time to shower, change, feed the dogs, and run out the door again. When I got to the coffee shop Margaret was sitting in her favorite chair sipping her coffee and had mine on the table next to her.

So, cougar how did it go this morning? You are insane. It was awkward, but Cole is picking me up at noon tomorrow to help him pick out furniture for his new house. Well, make sure you like it because you might have to look at it every day. Shut up! Margaret just smiled and gave a little roar. We laughed until our make-up ran down our cheeks on both of us.

I know I shouldn't feel weird, and I am working on that daily. Like my daughter gets a Brazilian wax job, I have never gone for one and it's growing in and getting rather uncomfortable. Margaret laughs; let's go after coffee and we will both get one. Really? Yep I can't let my bestie go without me, it will be a first for both of us. I haven't shown you my tramp-stamp. WHAT she screamed, now everyone in the shop was looking at us. Awkward Margaret, remember to use your indoor voice I said in a whisper. Yea well Nicole is a grown-up kid. I wonder why she didn't tell me. The tattoo looks really new and last summer I know she didn't have it. Maybe it was her way of trying to find herself. Well, this day is getting more and more interesting by the moment

Margaret smirked. Come on, Margaret grabbed my hand and said, we are getting waxed then lunch if we are able to sit afterwards.

Sitting in the restaurant with our legs spread under the table cloth, we ordered crab salad and a whole bottle of wine. Luckily, I had a bottle of Advil and took four while Margaret took five. She smiled and said we are now Women Warriors, because anybody who can go through that is definitely a Warrior. Yea I think they should have a warning notice that says, *Childbirth Is Painless Compared to Our Brazilian Wax Job*. After two bottles of wine we staggered out and went to our cars. Thanks Margaret so happy you're my bestie, we should do this again in four weeks. She laughed, you're not serious, are you? We will get some real pain meds first. Ok I am in.

When I got home, I let the dogs out. I was so very overjoyed that they already had a run for the day, because I did not think I was capable of even walking for at least a day or two.

I went to the crafting table and sorted the cards. All the cards would take up at least 10 of the poster boards. I got out my photo boxes and started sorting through them to see what pictures I wanted to put up. Finally, after two hours I had to sit down. The pain wasn't as bad. I looked around the room at the black poster boards, the cards, the photos. Why me? I thought about my medical files with the secret label YU. I miss my family, I miss having someone in the house to talk to, I feel so lonely. My tears kept me company for almost an hour.

I let the dogs in, and we all had dinner together in front of the TV. This is a once in a while thing; eating in the living room watching TV Max, so don't get used to it. I had to fill out my little booklet, it didn't have any space to put down what type of pain I was experiencing. Then I thought, anyone reading why I had pain would be laughing at me. It was getting late, so we went to bed, and I was a little happy we didn't have to get up early tomorrow.

The next day was sunny and a warm 52 degrees. I took a few Advil knowing I would be doing a lot of walking around the furniture store. Cole pulled up and I said good bye to the dogs and carefully got into his car. Are you feeling ok he asked? Oh, just dandy I said smiling.

We pulled up to the furniture store. I took pictures of the rooms, kitchen and floors. Smart man Cole, you impress me more and more. As we walked through the store a sales man greeted us. I explained that we were looking for living room, dining room, and bedroom. I asked about how long for delivery and were there any costs for bringing the furniture inside the house. He went to check on delivery dates.

We started with living room furniture. I found everything right away. There was a leather brown couch, a fabric recliner in cream and rustic chests for a coffee table. Cole was impressed. I can see what you mean about color and texture now. Ok, I have the model numbers, now let's find your dining room. Looking only took minutes. A long blonde wood table with a bench and chair combo. Now we need cushions I think we should do cream and blue square print. We need this buffet side board table also. We can match the cushion print for table runners on the table and side board. Thank you, Cole for brining me, this is so much fun. Ok Lisa, if this is fun then this is fun. I have all the model numbers lets go find a bedroom set.

So, Cole do you want soft, medium, or firm mattress. I would say medium. Ok do you want your bed to be able to raise up so you could read in bed. Yea, that sounds good. We found a king size bed that was electric. We lay down side by side and looked at each other. The sales man came over and said, this is a great bed. All the king sizes are firm. I am sure you will both love this bed then he walked away. We were silent for a very long moment. I guess since we are in bed together, he thought we were married. I laughed. Cole turned on his side to face me. Tell me Lisa, I noticed you are wearing wedding rings and you haven't in a year. Wow you are observant. I bought them when I was in

• • •
148

Amsterdam. I thought it could be a useful deterrent. Do you ever plan on getting married again? I looked at him and smiled then said, do you ever plan on getting married again? I would like to very much he said smiling. I would like too; eating is more fun when you have someone to talk to. My problem is I am not a very good cook. Well, I am still taking cooking classes, but I am a pretty good cook even if I say so myself. Oh no, does this mean we are being honest. He looked at me confused. I confess, I didn't make the blueberry pie or the sticky buns I got them at the bakery and used my own pie dish. He laughed at me and then kissed me on my nose. You make doing anything so much fun. I shoved him out of the bed and onto the floor laughing. So, mister they don't have the king in medium firm, but we can get egg-cushion pillow topper which will add another two to three inches on top. Let's also look at the head boards, I am thinking a bronze metal to blend with the flooring.

After another hour of haggling in free two-day delivery, and I had a 10% teacher discount we left the store. I should take you when I go buy a car. I can do that; Margaret and her husband always bring me when they get a new car. Really? Yep, really. Do you want me to go to your house on Tuesday and wait for the furniture delivery, I am good giving directions where everything should go? Yes, that would help a lot. I am trying not to use any sick days if possible, I have over 190 days. Wow, you are a super serious teacher, you never use your sick days.

How about we have an early dinner, I owe you for helping save money and furnish our house in style. How about we go to Zorro's. Yes, I love that place. As we drove, I thought about his comment "our house", maybe it was a slip of the tongue. Was Margaret right, did I have to like the furniture because I may see it every day. No, I was wrong he didn't like me like that, more as a friend.

After dinner, Cole dropped me off, I called Margaret and told her about my day. Well now, Margaret said in a smug tone, now that you two have been in bed together when is the wedding? He kissed me on top of my oily nose. I hope I don't have to start getting pimple cream too. Not that I should tell you he is dropping off his house key so I can wait for his furniture on Tuesday. Oh, ok Lisa and will you be arranging the furniture in your house. Stop it!

I filled out my little booklet, ate dinner, and got into my pjs and cuddled on the couch with the dogs. Ok, you two I have doctors' appointments tomorrow so we all will get up early, yes early. There was a knock on the door. I wasn't expecting anyone, and only a few people knew I was home. I went to the door and peered out to see Cole. I opened the door and he smiled. Cute pjs he said. Hey, don't make fun of my flying dogs. I brought over my house keys for you. He handed them to me. Great, thanks. There was a loud crash sound from the TV. I jumped. What are you watching? *Now You See Me.* Do you want to come in and watch it, it's a great movie? Sure, but I left my pjs home. Pjs not required. You are in luck it just started, and the butter is still warm on the popcorn. Cole found a spot in between Max and Bella and settled in. During a commercial he looked at both dogs. Lisa, your dogs are looking at me, I don't know if they are going to eat my popcorn or me. If you get enough butter on your hands, they will eat you. I put the dogs out and came back to sit down.

Lisa, I want to ask you something, but you don't have to answer, just tell me to shut up. Sure, what is it. You are wearing a head scarf; I was wondering that's all. If I took off my scarf you would jump up and run away, I look like Frankenstein. Let me see. What are we kids? He laughed. Ok, don't say I didn't warn you, even the dogs hide their eyes. I removed my scarf. I didn't look at him. My scar's redness was gone, and it was still somewhat visible, but hair was already covering parts. Wow, you look like that Irish girl singer. I laughed, yea I know who you mean. Cole, thanks you always say the right thing. Yea, that's me Mr. Wright. You really are Mr. Wright. He leaned over and kissed me gently on the lips. He backed up and said you have been through so much and you are still so beautiful inside and out. You are an amazing woman. I feel like a Warrior Woman, and chuckled. I reached out and put my hand on Cole's cheek and said, you, Cole are an amazing man and I am so happy you are in my life. Cole started leaning in and in that instant the dogs started barking, starling both of us so our heads bumped into each other. Ouch, I got up to let the dogs in. It was awkward, but I decided to leave my head scarf off. I spoke in a deep Irish accent, I was mostly Irish anyway, "would you be liking some whiskey". Wow you really got that accent down. I went to get us drinks and came back to see the dogs had taken over the couch with Max lying on Cole's lap. I sat down and gave him his drink. She likes you. I am very likable. We watched the movie and I feel asleep. Cole not wanting to wake me; turned off the TV and put a blanket on me then left.

I woke dazed, not sure where I was. Then I remembered we had been watching TV last night. I must have fallen asleep. I hope I didn't snore or sleep with my mouth open. Awkward. I got up let the dogs out and showered, dressed, and made breakfast. I think I am running almost neck to neck with the fluffiest eggs ever, I even made seconds. I didn't want to be late for my second meetings with the doctors. I grabbed my little booklet, and off I went to see Gertrude first. As I was driving, I realized I didn't have my note pad or any questions, well I thought at least I did part of my homework.

Could I say the puppy ate my note pad? I don't think she had a sense of humor. Oh; sugar sticks, I could just write down some lame questions. I stopped at a Walmart and ran it to get a composition book and a pen. Next time one of my students don't have their homework, I am going to give them a break.

I sat in the parking lot trying to think of random questions. Like, will my brain age faster when I am older, and will I have old peoples' concerns. How will my body be affected by having a menstrual cycle, since I was in menopause? What should I do if someone doesn't recognize me or vice versa? That was enough, so I practically jogged into the office. When I stepped into the office the receptionist said go right on in. Ok; not even enough time to catch my breath. I knocked on her door and heard her low gruff voice say, "Come in!" I came in and there she was standing next to her desk again. I wondered if she ever got a Brazilian wax. I tried not laugh. I handed her my booklet and she gave me a new one. She sat and took a few minutes to review my answers, then took a pen out and did some writing. Well, your ratings suggest you are having some stress in a normal range. Tell me did you write down any questions? Yes, I gave her the composition book?

After a minute she said, well most of these are more medical questions, but the last one is one we can address. Tell me more about this question. I told her about what had happened at the mall and how panicked I was and put my sunglasses on and left quickly. Gertrude looked at me and said very slowly, what do you fear that the girl would see your daughter instead of you? Yes, I would have to lie and say no, I am Nicole's mom, I practice talking in a higher pitch, so I don't sound like her. Do you think the girl would believe you? Yes, I think she would. Then you have nothing to worry about. But what if… Gertrude put up her hands and said STOP, we can't live our lives with "what ifs". The girl would most likely believe you; now that is solved. Most people will not argue with a grieving mother. Now, tell me what you would do if the girl didn't believe you? I thought for minute and finally said, I would say to her, "I miss her too". Gertrude looked pleased.

You are quite a remarkable person. I applaud you. Thank you; I said waiting for the bomb to drop. Do you have any other questions? No. Ok, then I will see you next week and please fill out the booklet. If you feel the need to call me or see me again this week, all you need to do is call and I will be available. You can call me at any time. She handed me her card with her personal cell phone number. You have an appointment with Dr. Light today. Yes, in about two hours from now.

I sat in my car and thought to myself, did she seem really extra nice, or was her speaking more softly which made her seem friendly. I couldn't decide. I had enough time to get something quick to eat at WAWA then get to Dr. Light's office on time with traffic.

When I got to Dr Light's office the woman behind the window, just waved me in. Dr. Light was coming down the hall with a big smile on his face. Ok, so you illuminate your smile because of your name. He laughed. He took my hand and asked how I was doing. I am doing good. I have a little surprise for you. First, we will run some tests I want to do a urine then blood tests. Surprise, I love surprises. When we reached his office, I saw test tubes already lined up. He walked over and handed me the bowl to fill. I looked at him and said a surprise would be not having to fill a bowl. After I returned with the bowl, he told me to sit. He did a few things then came over to take some blood. He did this very quickly and then handed me some orange juice. He went to his desk and worked on his computer, in seconds the large screens in his office lit up. One had Greta's face and the other Dr. Vinke. Oh, my I am so happy to see you.

While I spoke to them Dr. Light was busy with his tests. After about 20 minutes Dr. Light stood next to me and said; Greta you wanted to talk to Lisa. I looked at him then turned to face the screens. Dr. Vinke and Greta were both smiling. What; I said.

Greta said, Lisa you have shown so much resilience and bravery. Sometimes we don't understand why some things happened in our lives, but I know that you have that belief that it should make us stronger. Dr. Vinke would you like to share the news.

Dr. Vinke smiled and said we have good news for you. I know this will come as a shock to you, but I have had Dr. Light run more tests to confirm you are healthy and that you are pregnant.

Dr. Light grabbed a chair, and gently eased me into it. Umm are you sure, did you say I was having a baby? Yes, you are having a baby, and Dr. Light ran some test to check on the health of your baby and all is well. You are going to have a baby. I was in a state of shock and couldn't believe it, how is this possible?

Lisa, you are roughly about 4 to 5 weeks pregnant. Your daughter must have been only a few days pregnant when you had the accident. During your operation and the few days afterward, the fetus was in no danger of any of the medicines you had taken. Dr. Light did standard tests last week and that's when he discovered you were pregnant. He ran other various tests to check for anything in your system out of the ordinary. When you came in today, he ran another pregnancy test and others to test your hormones. From the smile on his face, everything is fine. I looked at Dr. Light and he took my hand and said congratulations.

Greta spoke softly, Lisa how do you feel? I turned and looked at Greta on the screen. Now that is a loaded question. I don't know, it's my baby's baby. I am a grandma and yet I am also giving birth. Greta, if I was confused before about who I am, now I; I don't even know how to finish this sentence. Lisa, you are you and you are having a baby. You are the mother to this baby. Congratulations Lisa. Yes, Mrs. Goodwin congratulations on your new baby. We both are signing off and will talk you soon, like next week. With that Dr. Light turned off the screens.

Dr. Light pulled his chair next to mine and took my hands into his. Tell me what's going on in your head. I don't know where to begin. I am happy that I will have my daughter's baby. I will have to retire, as it wouldn't look good, a single pregnant teacher. I keep reminding myself that my mind is well educated, not old, and my body is a fit 23-year-old. I could raise a child; I am not 44 years old. It's my grandchild and it's my child too. I looked at Dr. Light; well my house is not going to be quiet in 9 months. I am happy and something else, I don't know what, shock; I guess. Look, if you need to talk or ask questions you have my phone number. Also,

Gertrude knows also. So, we are here to support you in any way possible. I turned and looked at him and said, thank you. If you like in a month or so we can do an ultra sound. I guess we will see you next week.

On the drive home, I started thinking about Cole. What was I going to do? I didn't want to be alone the rest of my life, and he was a great guy, which are really hard to find. What would he say if I told him I was pregnant? Could I say I was mysteriously implanted? What am I going to do? I got home and let the dogs out. I called Margaret and said in a shaky voice I need to talk to you. I am on my way right now. No, no you can come after school. I am coming now, there is a student teacher next door I will get her and will be there in 20 minutes and hung up. Aww, it was pretty heavy news, now what do I do?

Margaret was here in 25 minutes with a covered pan in her hand. She pushed her way through and put the pan in the refrigerator turned around and grabbed me by my elbows. You went to the doctors today what happened?

We need to sit down for this conversation. Just then my cell phone I looked at it. It's Cole, I can't talk to him, please tell him I am just sad and overcome with grief and needed to talk to you, oh, and tell him I will be there tomorrow to make sure he gets his furniture. Margaret swiped the phone and told Cole that I was just sad; and she will be at your house tomorrow to wait for the furniture and have a home-cooked meal ready for you. Then she hung-up. What are you crazy, why would you tell him I will be at his house with a home-cooked meal? Don't worry, you have the Bitterballens I just put into your fridge.

Margaret, I think I am still in shock, and I still really don't know how to handle this situation with Cole. Tell me already will you! I am pregnant! Come on seriously, it isn't April Fools' Day tell me. I did, I am going to have Nicole's baby, she was a few days pregnant when we left. The doctor has run all kinds of tests and the baby is fine. I am about 4 to 5 weeks pregnant. I took my index finger on Margaret's chin and closed her mouth shut. I know it's insane; my life has been in an upheaval for over a year. We are not talking normal people upheaval we are talking SCI-FI out of this world weird. I am going to be a grandmother and a mother at the same time. Margaret how am I going to tell Cole. I really feel like we are into the relationship arena. What would I say to him; Oh, Cole, yes, I have feelings for you, and by the way I am pregnant, and I don't know who by, or when? Margaret say something please!

Margaret smiled; I just can't believe it. Nicole gave you the gift of life and another gift of life to cherish.

Oh, Margaret don't make me cry. I am not going to cry. She really did, and when you say it like that, I should be dancing around the room. You are going to give me a baby shower, right? I reached to her and we embraced. You are right Margaret; I didn't see it for what it is.

You will have to tell Cole the whole story, he is trustworthy. Yes, I know, but he may not want to get involved with a pregnant woman, and what would people say and his parents? You have to cross that bridge when you come to it. You have been through a lot, and you are still standing. You can do this. I don't know what Cole will do, but I know he is a good man and I think he thinks a lot of you.

Who is the father? I looked at her, I am not sure, but I would guess Sam. I haven't met him yet; I was going to meet him on spring break. I can't believe the jerk got my daughter pregnant. Hey, Margaret took my hand, remember it takes two. Yea right, he probably seduced her, or got her drunk. Lisa, you don't know that. Are you going to tell this Sam? I looked at her puzzled. Tell him what? That he is going to be a father. Margaret, I don't know if he is; first of all. I can't pretend to be Nicole now that everyone has been told she died in the crash. This is my baby and I don't want to drag out custody in the court system. I don't think it would come to that, but what about when the baby askes where daddy is? Lisa, if you were a mother, wouldn't you want to know? Margaret you always help me make sense of life, and sometimes I hate it when you are right.

More importantly, what do I say to Cole. Maybe you should talk to the "father" first and see what the situation is. After you KNOW what the situation is, you need to tell Cole everything. Yea, guessing and trying to figure out things makes my head hurt. I will go to the college Wednesday and get her stuff and see if I can find him.

See Lisa, focus on one thing at a time, see how easy that was. I hate you! Well, you won't anymore once you taste those Bitterballens I have perfected for you. Come on I made four dozen, well actually 7, I have some in my freezer. We sat in the living room eating. So, heat some of these and make some pasta in butter sauce and a salad with bread at Cole's house dinner done. I can't believe you hung up on him. Well, let's talk baby, baby, baby!

After Margaret left; I took the dogs for a run. We had dinner in the living room again. I have to stop this bad behavior, we would never let Nicole do it, I thought. I got out my little booklet. I filled it out in red ink. Some extreme emotional changes have taken place.

Then, I texted Cole, telling him I was fine and would see him tomorrow after school. He immediately texted back, glad you are ok, was worried, looking forward to dinner. Oh crap, I have to pick up dessert too.

We ran upstairs for bed time. Nudging both dogs over so I could have some room I got into bed. Bella lay her head on my belly. I stroked her. You hear it don't you? She gave a soft whine. Bella we will spend some time together soon. Max started tackling my arm and stood on my chest. Ok, time for peek-a-boo. I made a quick video, and checked on the ones I had made, wow, over 2,000 hits for the first and 909 for the other. We snuggled and slept with dreams of diapers and rattles.

We woke late and had breakfast and a long run. I wondered how long I could run while I was pregnant. I really enjoyed running. I have to find a new OB GYN doctor. I couldn't go to mine, I think he would notice that I had "changed" and so, I called a new doctor and made an appointment for Friday. I packed up some salad, bread, Bitterballens, and my laptop. I would stop at the bakery for cherry turnovers. Oh, dear I couldn't be drinking wine, so I also needed to pick up cider, soda and juice.

I finally got to Cole's house about 11:00 and unpacked everything. The furniture store said they would deliver from noon to two. I put my laptop on the kitchen counter and used my folding chair which I had left to sit on. I had to read my emails and update Facebook.

I still hadn't told my sister and brothers that I was home. I knew they would all be coming over and staying with me for a few days or a week. I love them dearly, but I needed alone time to get my life in order, if it would ever be in order. I told them that Margaret was organizing a memorial for Nicole for February 9th and that I would do my best to make there. I still felt bad, I tried to think of it as a white lie, because I really would do my best to be there; right!

I also emailed Crystal, Nicole's dorm mate, and told her I was coming up tomorrow to pick-up her things. I also let her know that if anyone could use her clothes or books feel welcome to them. She emailed me back in a flash. I thought do these kids now a days live on their phones. She said she already organized everything for me and had no classes, so she could help me. This would be a test. Crystal had grown up with Nicole and knew her well, as they lived together at college for the past 5 years. I would have to wear lots of makeup, baggy clothes that covered me completely. I would put my head scarf on maybe even over my ears. I would pick up some glasses.

That gave me an idea, I called the shop where I got my glasses and said I needed a pair of fake glasses for a play at school, and could they sell me a pair. Ralph the eye doctor said not a problem, he would leave a pair with the receptionist and I could pick them up at any time.

I was getting a little hungry and decided to get something to eat. I didn't want to go through his cabinets, so I opted for a couple Bitterballens and juice mixed with soda. I walked around the house trying to decide where all the furniture would look best. I could tell where the sun came through the windows, because Cole hadn't put up any curtains yet. I got back on my computer and looked up the Blinds to Go store website. I picked out wood blinds for the bedroom, and shades for the bathroom, and curtains for the living room. I put them in the "cart" and did a screen shot. I texted Cole and sent him the pic. I was actually getting excited about where to put the furniture.

The pounding on the door startled me. I opened it to find two burly men in uniforms smiling. I am glad they had uniforms on, or I would have shut the door quick. Morning ma am, we have the bedroom furniture at the end of the truck so we will start there. Great, let me show you where everything goes. These guys were fast and efficient and had the bed set up in 10 minutes. While they were unloading furniture, I went to my purse to make sure I had money for a tip for both of them. I had two fifties, and that would do.

After the men left, I looked around the house, it was so beautiful, I love it. I realized Cole didn't have any sheets for the king size bed, and place mats would be nice for now on the table with some flowers. So off to the store I went. I came back washed the sheets and made his bed. Then I set the table and started dinner because he would be here in less than 20 minutes. I heard his car pull up and went to the door to meet him. As he was getting out of the car, I yelled come on man, come and see your castle! He laughed. Wow you are really excited about this Lisa. Yes, I am, it was so much fun and we have to get throw rugs and pillows, and ...well sorry I just got carried away there. Come Sir Cole and see your castle.

While eating dinner, I said we should get a porch swing facing the park. Also, a metal grate for the stone fire place. Cole laughed, I am so glad you are enjoying this, and the place looks like a castle. Thank you so much for making this a castle and Lisa you did make this feel like home. Ready for some turnovers? While we ate, I asked Cole if he ever sat in the living room in front of the TV eating dinner. No, I haven't but I would like to try it if I had a TV. Humm you do need a TV. Will you come with me

Ms. Castle Designer this weekend and we can pick out a TV and order the blinds. Oh, and we need some area rugs, do you have any pictures to hang up? Nope but let's take one now for our first dinner. Now, how about joining me for dinner tomorrow night? Ok, sounds great. I need to get home to let the dogs out. Cole walked me to my car and said, hey bring the dogs with you tomorrow. Really you want them trampling through your castle. Yes, I do, it will make it cozy. He leaned in and kissed me, really kissed me. A car went by and honked its horn. Ok, that's enough public display. We both laughed and he kissed me on my nose, see you tomorrow about 4:30.

On the way home, I thought, how do you tell someone you're in your kid's body, and yea having your kid's baby too. The dogs were really happy to see me, no strike that, happy to be let outside. I let them out and called Margaret and told her about how Cole loved his castle and I was invited over for dinner with the dogs.

Margaret asked, are you still going to the college tomorrow? Yes, Crystal is going to help me, she said she already packed up everything. I am going to see if I can meet this Sam guy as well. What are you going to tell him? I really don't know. Like you said, we will cross that bridge when we come to it.

• • •

When I let the dogs in, they were the first to run upstairs. I got into bed with some nudges. I had to start getting into bed before the dogs did. Max was ready to play peek-a-boo. With her little girl voice, she said; "Why do they call it a litter of puppies? Because they mess up the house". I took her little paw and made her wave good bye. I posted it and checked on the other vids. The numbers were growing fast. I sent copies to Greta, Mr. Dupree, Margaret and Cole. Well, Max you are getting famous. Bella lay her head on my tummy and I curled up next to her.

We were getting lazy and again woke up late. I made breakfast and filled out the little booklet in red again. I got ready for a run and had to wake the dogs. We went for a long run. I knew I would be gone all day at the college. I got dressed and headed to my car when my phone buzzed. It was Cole texting me. The kids loved your video of Max. See you tonight Princess Lisa. I headed to my eye doctor and picked up the glasses waiting for me. Ok here we go. Maybe I should have a tissue ready to hide my face like I am crying which I probably will do any way.

I took a deep breath and had my tissue ready as I knocked on the dorm door. Crystal opened the door and flew into my arms hugging me tightly. I hugged her and rubbed her back. I miss her everyday too.

After about 30 minutes of crying, hugging, and blowing our noses we sat down. Tell me about Nicole's boyfriend, Sam. Crystal looked like she was going to cry again. Mrs. G this has been the worst few months of my life. I don't know how to tell you. I looked at her for a long moment, tell me what? Start from the beginning.

Well, Sam and Nicole have been friends for a few years, he was working on his Ph.D. and she was helping him for the past year. Nicole, I think was his first real girlfriend, they started getting really close about 8 months ago. He really loved Nicole and was so devasted when he heard about the plane crash it was really bad for him. He was going to propose to her on New Year's Eve. Crystal got up for more tissues and reached into one of the boxes on the floor and pulled out a velvet ring box. She handed it to me. I opened it to find a diamond that could only be described as a rock. He gave me the ring and asked me to give it to you. Why? Well there is more to the story. Sam was so crushed about Nicole; he called his parents and went to see them. His parents are in the Peace Corps in Africa. He was there only a week when the camp he was in was hit with missiles. Sam and his parents were; didn't make it. We sat in silence. I put the ring on my right hand. I looked at her and said diamonds last forever and their love fills the earth with flowers. I am so, I don't know. I feel like I have lost a son-in-law. Crystal took my hand. Sam said he wanted you to have it, because their happiness together shone as bright as the diamond. There was a memorial service for him and his parents almost two weeks ago. Most of the kids here at college went and his family. He had three sisters and their families. There were well over 500 people who attended. Even the mayor was there and some folks from the Peace Corps also.

Wow, life is delicate and the adventure it takes you on has many trials. These trials can make you bitter or better. Their love together was cut short but will be remembered in our hearts and should bring us a smile; not tears. We sat holding hands in silence for a long time.

Finally, I got up and sat on the floor next to the boxes. Crystal said, I know some girls who could use some clothes, and definitely her books. The small box has her jewelry, blankie, and photo album. There is one photo album with lots of pictures of her and Sam. This is the only box I want. I hope the rest can be used. Crystal walked me to my car and placed the box on the back seat. I will see you on the 9th of February. Mrs. G one more thing, some of us were wondering if in May you would walk in the graduation and accept Nicole's degree. It would mean a lot. I have the number for grad office, and they have already said yes. I will text you the information. I hugged Crystal for a long time. Nicole's life was rich with a friend like you Crystal.

On the way home I had to pull over a few times. It was so unbearable this grief I had been suffering for a year. I had to pull myself together. When I was really sad; I used to think about people who suffered much more than me. I thought about Sam and his family and the people in the refugee camps who lost so much in their lives. I had friends, a home, Bella, a puppy, a job as a teacher, a boyfriend and baby on the way. When I got home, I got the box from the back seat and went in. I let the dogs out and went to Nicole's room. I took out her blankie and wrapped myself in it and took a nap.

At four, I got dressed and texted Margaret and told her I would call her later when I got home. I got the dogs and we went to Cole's. Over dinner I told Cole about my trip to the college and about Sam. I showed him the ring. I feel like I have lost my son-in-law. He would have married Nicole and had children. Also, I am going to walk in the graduation in May and get her degree. Then we talked about what Cole needed for his castle. Dinner was great and this time I kissed Cole. I could really get used to you making dinner. Well then, he said with a smirk, there is Thursday and Friday we will go out to eat. Really, you are the best Cole. We took the dogs out for a walk along the park path which was well lit.

Cole took my hand and we walked quietly around the path three times. When we got back to his house, I said thank you for letting me bring the dogs. Nonsense they are part of the package deal. I love these pups, and always wanted one. Well if that's the way you feel, would you like to dog sit Max, I want to spend some time with Bella on Sunday.

Great wolfie and I get to spend some time together. Maybe we can do a video. I laughed so loud, I stopped when he just stared at me. Ok, maybe that was a little too loud. Cole guffawed and said, do you want me to come to your place tomorrow to rid your home of healthy foods? Yea, that would be good. We can watch TV while we eat in the living room! Whoa I have never done that. There is a first time for everything. Cole kissed me deeply and I might add somewhat passionately before the dogs started barking at us.

When I got home; I called Margaret and told her about what had happened at the college and over at Cole's Castle. Wow, Lisa I am so sorry. Do you want me to come over? No, I have cried so much today my tear ducts are swollen shut. I will see you Saturday. I am getting so tired. Babies do that to you.

My days were so busy. I was so tired, we all curled up and slept. I woke in the middle of the night and couldn't get back to sleep. I went into Nicole's room

• • •
171

and sat on her bed and opened the photo album. Looking at the pictures made me smile and cry at the same time. Two young people with their whole life ahead of them. Yet neither one knew what they left behind in this world. Nicole had given me the gift of life and another precious gift of life to cherish. I would make sure her baby would be cherished every day of his or her life. With her blanket wrapped around me I slept.

The dogs found me in the morning and barked at me. Ok, really is that your good morning? I let the dogs out and made a double batch of eggs. I was just hungry and tired. Tomorrow I would be going to the doctor's office. I have to keep reminding myself that I am not 44; I am 23 now. When I was pregnant with Nicole, I had only gain 19 pounds and really didn't show that much. I had always worn loose fitting clothes, as I was maybe a size or two above what I should be. I hoped that would be true now. I would have to retire and stay home and play with baby. Yea, I liked that. I took the dogs for a run and came home. I showered and changed. I wanted to pick up some TV dinner tables and dessert too. By the time I got home is was almost 4:30. I let the dogs out and set up the new TV tables and laid out the spices and dishes.

When Cole pulled up, I opened the door and almost said welcome home honey, but it was too soon for that. The dogs were excited as Cole came in carrying a bag. What do you have? Secret for after dinner. He had dinner plated with 15 minutes. We ate our dinner in front of the TV watching the news. I looked over at him and shoved him with my shoulder. We look like an old couple sitting around the TV.

After we finished, Cole took the plates and said, you stay here for the surprise. What did you get for dessert, I will bring that out too? Cheese strudel! 10 minutes later Cole came out with the dessert and mugs of coco with different colored marshmallows. What is this? I ordered them from France. They are flavored marshmallows. The coco is from there also, it's a type of mint. Now this is living large. The flavors are so good, I love this, it is now officially my favorite food in the world, and you are my favorite person.

We watched a movie then took the dogs for a quick walk. I have to head home I have some school homework to do, I will pick you up at 5:30 tomorrow for dinner. Ok, I will see you then. He kissed me and waved good bye.

I went upstairs to change into my Pjs. Then I started to head down the stairs, and the dogs raced ahead of me all the way down the stairs, I turned and literally jumped into my bed. I pulled up the covers and laughed. The dogs seemed to realize that they had been double crossed and came tearing up the steps. I was laughing so hard my stomach hurt. Bella was insulted and got on the bed and turned her back to me. Poor Max was yelping to get up and after many attempts, she got up on her own. I was too busy laughing to help her.

In the morning I let the dogs out and made breakfast. I never really cooked in the mornings because I had to work. I was getting pretty good at it. I had the OB-GYN appointment today. Then I had to decide what to wear for dinner. I could wear one of my new outfits the one with the matching scarf and purse.

I headed out to the doctor's office, nervous, why, I had been through this before. He can't see my brain. He would just think what. Oh no, I thought; can he tell how old I am by looking so intimately at my body. Can a 44-year-old look like a 23-year-old? I couldn't use my insurance card; how would I pay for a $20,000-dollar birth? Ok, I need to breathe, focus on one thing at a time. Why couldn't I have a nice bod? I am 44 and take really good care of myself that's all. I think it's teeth that they can tell how old you are. I have to write down this question. Ok breathe, no need to panic. I had to get through this.

When I got to his office, the receptionist had me fill out about 5 pages along with my drivers' license and insurance card. I went into the back and was given a gown. I waited for 10 minutes, but it seemed like an hour. The doctor came in smiling with his hand outstretched. Hello, I am Dr. Lavis I read over your file, and I just want to check some information. You are 44 years old; you don't smoke, you are a teacher. May I ask how your health is, you checked off no on all the boxes, but I notice you are wearing a head scarf. Yes, I was in an accident and some bones in my skull cracked. No big deal. I was home within days. They shaved my head and my hair hasn't grown back yet. I should have thought of this before I came. So, what brings you here today? I think I am pregnant! Ok, let's take a quick urine test then examine you. He did the urine test and said yes you are pregnant. You didn't put down when your last period was. Do you remember? Oh, life has been so hectic the holidays the accident, maybe a month ago? Now sweat was dripping my down the side of my face.

Ok let's do your exam. Well you keep yourself in good shape. Oh, I run daily, can I continue running. Sure, until it gets uncomfortable for you. Have you been trying to get pregnant? No, it just happened. How long have you been sexually active? Not very long. Everything is in perfect shape and you apparently take very good care of yourself. It appears you are about 5 to 6 weeks pregnant.

He finished and put my legs down and asked me to sit up. Mrs. Goodwin do you know what your plans are? I plan to have the baby. Ok, that is great. We need to discuss setting up a date for various tests such as chorionic villus sampling and an amniocentesis. Due to your age you are categorized as a high-risk pregnancy. Do you understand what I mean by a high-risk? Yes, doctor, various types of chromosomal abnormalities like down syndrome, trisomy 21, and having older eggs. My chances of having a DS is 1 in 19. I don't have many new mothers who are that informed. We don't have many first -time mothers who are 44 either. I also want you to be mentally prepared for the rigors of bringing this pregnancy to full term at your age. I have a number to a woman therapist who specializes in high-risk.

Your muscle tone is quite strong. Do you exercise a lot? Yes, I eat very healthy most days, lots of blueberries every day, and running. The blueberries are very good for you, keep that up. I am going to give you some vitamins which you should take daily. They will make your hair grow faster. If you want to keep your hair-do down there you can until your ninth month. I had to laugh which finally put me at ease.

The nurse will be in after you change and will give you the vitamins. The receptionist will set up your next appointment. On the appointment card is my emergency phone number do not hesitate to call me at any time of the day or night. Do you have any other questions or concerns? Yes, I do, I paused then said, why can't every OB GYN be as kind and as good looking as you! He laughed; I will see you next month.

When I got into my car; I threw my arms up in triumph. I was sweating bullets, but I did it. I lied on the forms not checking off widowed or had a live birth before. I didn't think the insurance company read those, or at least I hoped not. I could always say I was nervous and forgot, who wouldn't being pregnant. I am not a good liar, and I really feel the guilt of it. These deceits were for what, so no one would know I had a body transplant. Think of the news media and what would happen to my life. Nope not going to think about that. I am going home and get ready for a date. Humm a pregnant woman getting ready for her first date.

I was ready and really looked good if I do say so myself. Cole came early and he even opened the car door for me. On the way to the restaurant Cole looked at me. Why are you staring at me? You look so fabulous and glowing with beauty. Oh boy I would have to tell him soon. Tonight, is for me. Thank you, Cole, you are always charming and handsome which makes all the girls hate me. He laughed, then said, really. Yes really.

We had Mexican food which I love steak Tampiquena. It was a wonderful night. We were both relaxed and the conversation flowed as if we had been a couple for years. We sat in the restaurant for over two hours, then went to the coffee shop and sat for almost three hours. When we got home, we kissed for over a half an hour and felt giddy. I will see you Sunday about noon, we will look for a TV and window treatments. What did you just say Cole, window treatments? Yea, that's what the catalog calls them. Ok.

I let the dogs out and while they were out, I changed into my Pjs. I put two dog treats next to my bed. I texted Margaret and asked her to get blueberry muffins with our coffees tomorrow. I filled out my little booklet, still in red. I let the dogs in, and they headed upstairs. I went up with them then called them and started going down stairs, and they fell for it again, as soon as they were rushing down the stairs I jumped into bed. The little pitter-patter of Max's feet were so cute. Bella looked disgusted and leaped on the end of the bed. Max had master getting up on the bed. We played peek-a-boo and in Max's really silly and still laughing voice said, "What do snowman call their off-spring? Chill dren"! We posted it and sent it to Greta, Mr. Dupree, Margaret and Cole.

I love Saturdays, get up late, meet with Margaret for a couple of hours then do whatever I need to, like not cleaning, not cooking, not laundry and play for the rest of the day. Margaret was there waiting with some blueberry muffins. I told her about our date, then about how I was panicking at the doctor's office. The doctor asked if I was sexually active and how *strong* my muscle tone was. I didn't answer the question about having a live birth or widowed. Don't worry, cross that bridge when you come to it. I told her about the testing he wanted to do since I was 44 and a high-risk pregnancy. You don't have to do the testing. I know. What am I going to do about going to the dentist? I can't put down I am 44 he will know I am not. I think you need to call your friend Dr. Light. Yea, I think I will. Now I have to worry about how and when I am going to tell Cole. Well, honey, I think you had better do it soon. I showed her my ring that Sam had gotten Nicole. He was a good man. Maybe tomorrow after we go shopping, I will tell him. I also have Grief Group on Tuesday; I have to pick up the puppy for grumpy Sam. I didn't think about that I know two guys named Sam now.

Margaret looked at me, and then said, why did you choose to be you instead of Nicole? I think the biggest reason is I felt like I would have to lie every day to everyone. Also, I am going to retire and really don't want to work for another 30 years. I got my 25 years in and I want to enjoy life. Plus, I would really miss our Saturdays together, well I wouldn't lie to you. I couldn't use Nicole's degree in biochemistry what she does is complicated. I am starting to look forward to having this baby. If the baby is a girl are you going to name her, Nicole? I don't know, I think if she is a girl, she should have her own name. If the baby is a boy, I will name him Stone. I just love that name for a boy. So, what do you want to do for your Birthday on the 9th of February? Having the memorial is what I want to do. You did get gluten-free snacks? Yes, of course.

When I got home, I took the dogs for a run and then showered and changed into my Pjs. I had to pay some bills. Before I had left for our trip in December, I had paid all the bills for January and more on my credit card. When I went to my on-line banking; I couldn't believe the balance. Oh, yea, it dawned on me they must have put the money in from the airline insurance company. I had just over $180,000 in my checking account. Well baby we can start planning your college fund. Just think baby, when you are 20, I will be 65 in brain only. I hope I won't be a cranky old lady. Maybe old people are cranky cause they don't feel good and their bodies aren't what they used to be.

• • •

I went into Nicole's room and decided this would be for the baby. I had already cleaned out all the drawers. I emptied out her desk, closet, and shelves and put the bags of trash out. The only thing left were spare sheets for the bed. Then I started on the closets downstairs. I would need lots of room for a baby. I got rid of lots of things around the house, and old knick-knacks around the house. We didn't need any choking hazards. I had gotten rid of 7 bags of items stuff outside on the porch. I need to look forward.

I went upstairs and fell asleep in Nicole's bed with her blankie. When I woke in the morning, I lay in her bed thinking how my heart just ached. I missed my baby girl. I would have to tell Cole everything. I don't know how weirded out he would be. I got up and looked into my bedroom and saw both dogs still sleeping on my bed. I went downstairs and had breakfast. When the dogs smelled the bacon, they came running downstairs. Yea, no; you're not getting any, I let the dogs outside. I was so tired, but I knew I had to go running just to wake myself up. We did an extra-long run. I didn't know how long I would be at Cole's Castle today.

At noon Cole knocked on my door. Ok I am ready; let's go find a TV fit for a castle. He laughed, yes Princess Lisa. After we ordered the window treatments and got the TV, we picked up a dozen tacos to go. While sitting at Cole's table, you know I really miss having tacos. I haven't one in a long time. I can see that Lisa; I don't think I have ever seen a woman eat seven tacos in a row. Oh, sugar stick, I was only supposed to six, sorry Cole. Well, you owe me now. Ok! I looked at Cole and knew I had to tell him before we sat on the couch and something else distracted us.

Cole, do you still have that chocolate chip truffle ice-cream? I picked up two more yesterday; why? Well I am going to need one with a spoon, no bowl. Ok then. He got up and grabbed two spoons and the ice-cream and sat.

I have to tell you a couple of really shocking unbelievable SCI-FI type things that have happened to me. I don't know how they will affect our relationship. I know I can trust you will not tell anyone; we have known each other for years and you should know. Does this have to do with the plane crash and why you look 20 years younger? Yes, it is, but it's a little more complicated than that. Is it like a time-warp? No, not really, after eating three bites of ice-cream, I said, it's a case of donor surgery on foreign soil.

I told Cole everything, even about me being pregnant with my grandchild. Later, the second ice-cream was finished, and two hours passed, we sat licking our spoons.

Cole, how do you feel about me? Well, I think if I ask you now, you should say yes! Yes, to what? Will you marry me? A long pregnant silence. You already know how I feel about you. I would give you a ring, but you seem to already have plenty. You want to marry me knowing I am pregnant? Yes, and you should say yes, because we could be a family. The baby needs a father, and I would love to be a father and a husband to you. I do love you Cole, if at any time you feel like it's too weird or whatever it's ok, I will understand, I have been living weird for a month now. This seems too good to be true after all that has happened to me. Princess Lisa, you need a happy ending. Do you really mean it? Yes, I do! You haven't said yes yet. Yes, yes, yes, yes, I do. We held hands and sat smiling at each other for a long time. What will your family think?

We can get married soon if you want. This way people will think the baby is mine. Oh, yikes people will think you knocked me up and decided to marry me or that I trapped you into marry me. People will say and think things no matter what we do. Are you sure you want this? Yes Lisa, I wanted you for a long time.

Ok, just thinking outside the box, first could we use the ring that Sam was going to give Nicole. Sure. We can look for matching bands. We could apply for the license tomorrow, also we could do a wedding registry today; so, people think it was somewhat planned. We can have the mayor marry us on Valentine's Day. I could rush order invitations. We could get married where. Cole laughed, how about school. We could use the stage and the cafeteria for a buffet. We are going to have to have it catered, I love the cafeteria ladies but not their food. Ok, where is your laptop, we can reserve the faculties for that day. What time? Let's do 4:00. We could get Charlie to DJ, yes, he is hysterical, I couldn't imagine anyone else. Ok, reserved the stage and the cafeteria. Now, I will email Charlie. Ok, that's done. I will send an email to the mayor with the time and place and ask for confirmation.

Now, let's do the wedding registry, help me pick out what you need to cook with. Oh, does this mean I am the cook. Yea, do you want to eat what I make? Good point, I shoved him, and he shoved me back and we laughed. After another hour the wedding registry was done, and the invitations were done and on hold. We are going to get married! This is really happening! Ok, if I call Margaret everyone will know by tomorrow morning. Go for it. Wait, who will we get to cater? Who will be your Best Man, Mike I take it? Of course, Margaret and do we want to have more in the wedding party? I could ask my brothers, and would you want to have my sister also? Yes, and my sister too. Ok I will call her.

Margaret, hi what are doing? Oh, just waiting for you to call and tell me about what happened at Cole's Castle. You are on speaker and I am here with Cole. Maybe you should have started with that next time. Cole's Castle, I like it. Awkward. Anyway; Margaret, I need you to organize decorations and a caterer for Valentine's Day at school about 4:00. Decorations on the stage and gluten-free food in the cafeteria. Are we having a Valentine's Day party? No, Cole and I are getting married? A short pregnant pause. OMG, really oh, that is so wonderful, am I in the wedding party. Yes, of course you are. Ok, I know just who to get for gluten-free food, oh and my niece in Maryland is a Wedding Planner who takes care of everything the day of the wedding and makes sure everything runs smoothly. What? This will be her first one, but she is very thorough. When did Cole ask you? Cole answered, I asked her today and she said "yes, yes, yes, yes, I do." This is so wonderful, Lisa you deserve to be happy, so be happy. Thank you, Margaret. You can count on me.

So, do you have any type of theme in mind or colors? How about red, white, and pink since it's Valentine's Day. Let me give you the wedding registry address. We thought if we did a registry; people would think this was more planned and not like entrapment. Good thinking girlfriend! Cole said, what are you talking about. Cole, all those women out there eyeing you will think I entrapped you if they knew I was pregnant besides they are jealous too. I have the invites made along with registry address, but I just want to confirm with the mayor first. We will apply for the license tomorrow. Ok, Lisa this gives me two and half weeks, yes, we can do this no problem. Now, I am going to start on planning the decorations. Thank you so much Margaret I will talk to you later.

Wow, I need to get home to finish the photo boards, I wanted to make a few with Nicole and Sam. So, what time do want to go get the marriage license? How about I take the day off we will go in the morning and I will go to my doctor's office for the necessary blood work and signatures, you have your doctors' appointments, and when you get back we can have everything we need and go back with all the forms signed. You are going to take a day off from school? Wow, I must be special if you are taking a day off. Yes, you are, and he kissed me a long time. So, I am just making a list in my head, I need to put my house up for sale, and my sister and brothers will probably want to stay at my place for the memorial in a week and a half. Ok, slow down. Déjà vu struck me like a ton of bricks sitting on my chest. That is exactly what Richard, my husband used to say to me. Lisa are you listening you look far off. What?

Tomorrow we get the license. See if the mayor sends you confirmation and Charlie too. Tuesday you are going to pick up the puppy for grumpy, no; now you have me calling him grumpy Sam. You have over a week till the memorial, then another five days till we get married. If your family stays with you for both that's great, I can bring the dogs here so you have more room and it will give them a chance to settle in. Why are you so perfect? I am aren't I!

Once home, I felt like my head was swirling. There was so much to do and to think about. NO, stop it, I will focus on one thing at a time. Tomorrow. I let the dogs out. Then went to the bathroom mirror. Hey kid, what do you think about your mom getting married again? **Mom you are a princess and you really do deserve a happy ending. I love that you are going to use the ring Sam got for me. Just relax, check off the items on your list, enjoy the moments of now. Cole isn't dad, but I know that dad would be really happy to see you happy. Cole will take care of you and our baby. I love you mom, be happy.** I love you too baby-girl.

I texted Margaret then Cole. I was so excited how could I sleep. I let the dogs in. I decided to finish the poster boards tonight. After finishing them, I sent emails to my sister and brothers letting them know about the memorial and the wedding. I sat down and revised my list. Would I wear a wedding dress since this was my second wedding? I wasn't showing yet. I hoped I wouldn't get pregnant big like my sister did. Nicole had the same body frame I did, but that didn't mean anything, so did my sister. Focus, I need to get a dress. Should the wedding party be dressed the same? No, this would be casual. Red shirts for the men. Pink dresses for the girls. Oh, I wanted to call Margaret, but it was already one in the morning and she had to go to school. Finally, I gave up and curled up with what room that was left on the bed with the dogs.

We got up early did a really quick run and I dressed. I had to fill out my little booklet so Gertrude wouldn't get mad. Cole texted me and was on his way to pick me up. He asked if I had my birth certificate and other marriage papers.

When he pulled up, I was already out the door. He opened the car door for me. Playing hooky! He laughed. Most people in a small town know most people. So, when we went into the court clerk's office, we knew most of the people. Shelly the clerk, said so you two are getting married it's about time. How did you know? It seems the mayor got an email asking if he could marry you two at the school on Valentine's Day, that is so romantic. Cole said, we had planned to do this around Christmas time, but things got in the way. I looked at him and smiled. That bit of info would-be all-over town within 48 hours. Well here is your paper work, you need to sign here and here and here. I know you both, so I don't need to see all that other stuff. You need blood tests and doctor's signature bring them back and you got your license. Now, Cole I have to tell you that my granddaughter just loves you and thinks you are the best teacher in the world. Her grades used to be C's and now she is getting A's. You have made such a difference in her life. Thanks, it's heartwarming to hear that kids love learning.

Cole dropped me off at home and kissed me for a very long time in the car. Ok, I need to go to my doctors' appointments and get these forms signed. What time do you want me to come back, we can drop the papers off at the court clerk's office and I will make you dinner? I should be back by two. See you then, Mr. Wright. See you then Mrs. to be Wright.

Once in Gertrude's office, I had to tell her that I was getting married and that I had told Cole everything. We talked for a little more than our usual 45 minutes. As Gertrude walked me to the door, she took my hand and said be happy and don't worry, just be happy and live in the now. I hugged her. She wasn't as warm and welcoming like Greta, but I could see from her smile, she probably didn't get many hugs.

Along the way to Dr. Light's office, I stopped for some tacos and wolfed them down. When I went into Dr. Light's office, I saw that he had the screens on and both Greta and Dr. Vinke were on. I have some news for you all! After 20 minutes of chatter and congratulations, they had to go. Dr. Light filled out my paper work for me while I filled the bowl. Then he took more blood. I told him about my visit to the OB GYN and how I didn't think I would survive. He laughed, then apologized, it's just the way you tell something is so funny. Ok, so what do I do about a dentist? I will look into it for you and get the information to you within a few days. I also told him about visiting the college and how Crystal didn't recognize me as Nicole. I felt comfortable talking to Dr. Light, he made no judgements, just listened.

I made it home by 1:15, I took the dogs for a quick walk, then put the finishing touches on the poster boards. I thought about the slide show Cole had when his wife and daughter had died. I wanted to do a slide show during the reception about our lives and they were a part of it. I grabbed my flash drive and heard a knock on the door.

Hey Cole, I have all my papers signed. He laughed; in a hurry to get married! Yea, I have a bun in the oven. As we drove to the court clerk's office, I told him about my idea for a slide show. He loved it. He took my hand and said, I love you and every day you make me love you more.

When we got to the office, the mayor happened to be there talking to the clerk. Well, here comes the happy couple. I am looking so forward to marrying you both. I also am glad you are doing it at the end of day. I have three other couples who want to get married that day. Wow, you keep busy. I always clear my calendar on Valentine's Day. The mayor said, let me have your phone I will take a picture when the clerk hands you your marriage certificate. Great, thank you so much.

On the way back to Cole's house, I received a text from Charlie who was more than happy to DJ and said no charge to the happy couple. Cole laughed; we will get him a gift. Oh no, I didn't think about that, we have to get gifts for the wedding party. Did you call your family yet? Yes, I did last night and they; well as my mom put it; overjoyed. What did your sister and brothers say about being in the wedding party? They were going to beat me up if they weren't.

How many people are we inviting do we have a limit? Well, my family I have 32 which includes kids. Also, three friends outside of school, so 35 for me. I have 19 family. So, that's 54 and the 40 to 50 at school. I will order 120 just in case. I went online to the cart and paid for the invitations with the matching thank you cards along with a hefty fee for one day shipping. Which gave me an idea for making the wedding sign in book.

When we got to Cole's house, he opened my car door. Thank you, Cole, you are a real gentleman. Cole, I have my flash drive I need to put the slide show on and your list of people who are coming to the wedding so I can make mailing labels. Our school friends I will just put their name on, no need to mail them. Sounds like a plan on your list.

Cole started dinner for us. Ok Cole what is your password for your computer. It's "Coles Castle". I really liked that, so I changed it the other day. I laughed a little too loud. I was still getting used to having a different voice.

We ate dinner, and I updated my list. I was just thinking; I will call the women's shelter and have them come and donate most of my household furniture. Wow, that is a great idea. I called and set up a time for them to come on Wednesday with a really big truck. Lisa you are so kind and always thinking of others. I have cleaned out my house last year. I cleaned it out when I came home, and again the other day thinking I needed more room for the baby. There isn't a lot left. I went a little overboard and got rid of a lot I was just so sad and didn't want any reminders.

While Cole cleaned up, I sent an email to the realtor who I had gone to school with and told her I wanted to sell my house. Ok, I rounded up all your families' addresses, and you have a two or three other friends. Yea, I will hand deliver them. Try to get their address so we can send thank you notes.

Ok, Lisa tomorrow we have grief group and you're getting the puppy too? Yep, this will be so much fun. Do you want to tell the group we are getting married? Sure, I can do that. Alrighty, I will let you do that, then later I get to tell them I am pregnant. That's another twelve people we need to invite.

So, I need to complete the mailing labels, create the sign in book, order the supplies for favors tonight. Cole took my hand and kissed it. Hey, Mrs. to be Wright, slow down. Just focus on tomorrow. We have the place to get married, food and decorations via Margaret, DJ Charlie, the Marriage License with Mayor marrying us. The invitations and thank you cards on their way, by Wednesday or Thursday. We have a lot done in a matter of 48 hours.

I know, but a few items on my list can I run by you. Ok go ahead. Well, I was wondering the wedding party, the men wear dark red shirts, the women wear pink. Just then my phone rang. It was Margaret.

Yes Margaret, I have you on speaker. Hey happy couple, I have the wedding planner, my niece, set up and she will meet with you February 3rd during our coffee time, so Cole you can come to. Your gluten-free food is ordered along with appetizers for 100 to 110 people. The caterers bring the food, set up the food, serve the food, clean up the food and they will be wearing red aprons and black outfits. The women in the group will wear black pants with white shirts and red aprons. Red table cloths and heart shaped candles. We will have heart confetti all over the tables, I know how Lisa just loves confetti. I do and you aren't still mad at me for what I did last year all over your classroom. No, of course I am not mad I just couldn't teach for two days cause the kids were still picking up and playing with the confetti bomb you shot off in my room. That was funny, Cole started laughing, I remember that. Anyway, Jessie is helping with the decorations for the stage and the art teacher is helping with the cafeteria. We have it covered, no worries. I love you Margaret, let me know how much and if I need to make a deposit and such.

No worries, I have already checked your wedding registry and almost half of the items are bought. What how is that possible? News travels fast around here. I think Jessie is already planning your wedding shower. What? Oh, sorry you are not supposed to know that, scratch that, forget I said anything. I laughed. Talk to you later.

Let's get you home and you need to rest little mama. Ok, that sounds good to me. I will come tomorrow and pick you and the puppy up. Also, I am bringing cookies and a banana bread loaf, so you don't need to bring anything, I got this. Wow, you are a great man. We sat in the car kissing when finally, it was getting a little too cold. Bye Mr. Wright. Good night Mrs. to be Wright.

When I got inside; I let the dogs out and got onto the computer. I order heart chocolates in heart ceramic boxes with a photo slot on top. I couldn't decide if I should put a picture or just a note in the slot. I left it blank. I would set them in front of each chair wrapped in pink tulle with red ribbon and candy conversational hearts. Then I started on the wedding sign in book. I put pictures and quotes on each page and had to again pay a hefty price for one-day shipping. I though, I could justify the cost by; you only get married once, but that's not the case. I hadn't told Cole about the money I had gotten. I wanted to buy him a new car. I knew what kind he wanted and the color. I was thinking I could have it decorated for when we leave the wedding and drive off as husband and wife. I printed out the mailing labels. Shopped for his car. The Lexus dealer had a few in stock. I sent an email inquiry. They knew me well, as I have bought all my cars there and had them serviced for the past 18 years.

I let the dogs in. Sorry my little chilly dogs. Let's go to bed, mama is tired. We ran up the stairs. I got into bed and petted Bella until Max tackled my arm. I settled Max in for a video, we played peek-a-boo, and her joke was; "What kind of dog did Dracula have? A Bloodhound!". Max waved her little paw good bye. I checked the hits on the other vids, one had over 15,000 hits. The others were under five thousand. Nicole was right they are a hit or rather Max is a hit. We all got comfortable, well the dogs did, and off to sleepy land we went.

We woke up late and I took the dogs for a long run. I got back and changed. I had a double portion of eggs and toast. I called the breeder about picking up the puppy today. It would take about two hours there and back. I left before nine and stopped at the bank to get some money.

The realtor called while I was on the road, I asked her if she could stop by Wednesday. The Lexus dealership called, and I told them about my plan and that I would be in the following week. I was getting really excited about the puppy and I really hoped that grumpy Sam would be to. Otherwise, we would have three dogs.

Two hours later, I was heading home with the cutest, well, second cutest puppy ever! The puppy was so tiny, and the breeder said she would only be about 4 to 6 pounds full grown. The puppy actually fit in the palm of my hand. I stopped by the pet store and picked up a book on puppies, collar, tags, lease, food, bowls, and a tiny dog house bed.

When I got home; I made sure puppy did her business outside. I opened the back door and let the dogs out. Ok, girls, she is only here to visit. Puppy was not shy at all and jumped on Max. I let them stay out since it was warm day and the sun was shining a nice 55 degrees.

I started on the slide show for our wedding. I inserted my photos from the time I was little and family photos of Richard and Nicole. I added music and animations. I wanted to add more photos of Cole and me. I had to start taking pictures of both of us.

I brought the dogs in and puppy was tired. Puppy curled up next to Bella and Max pushed her way in. Cole pulled up with Chinese take-out. I took a picture of him. What are you doing? I need current pictures of us for the slide show. Oh, yea, that makes sense. We sat down and he put the chopsticks in his nose and said how about this one? Sure, thing Cole we all can wait to see sticks coming out of your nose, hold it, smile. Let's get one with our heads together, but I don't want my scarf showing. We took some more pictures. Then Cole saw the puppy. It's so tiny when was it born; yesterday. He picked up the puppy who was still asleep. So cute I almost want to keep her. I have the food and bed in my car we can take my car tonight. I will let her out so she can play some more and go to the bathroom again, we want her to sleep the rest of the night. We put the dogs outside again and I made sure that puppy went. Cole was cleaning up and I had to get some more pictures.

It was time to go, Cole went to get his cookies and bread and opened the passenger side door for me. I can drive while you hold the puppy. We put the puppy's front paws on the steering wheel and got a picture of her and Cole.

We got there before most people. Hey, do you see grumpy Sam's car? Yes, it's over there. Looks as old as him. Yea it does. That gave me another idea. Let's put the dog stuff next to or in his car if it's open.

We went inside, there were a few people setting up more chairs and snacks. Sam was sitting alone. I sat next to him and put my bag in between us. He looked over at me and said did you bring your friend. Ahh, Sam I didn't I am sorry, but I did bring a new friend for you to take home. He looked in my bag, I don't see anything. I lifted with one hand the tiny sleeping puppy and put her into his hands. Sam, this puppy needs a home. She won't get very big only about 4 to 6 pounds. She needs someone to take care of her. He held the puppy to his chest, and she opened her eyes and made a soft puppy sound.

Cole leaned over and said. Sam, I put some dog food and a dog bed and other stuff in your car. The paperwork for the puppy is in the envelope on your seat. I put the blanket on Sam's lap, and he lay the puppy on it, stroking it softly.

More people came in, and Lula clapped her hands and asked everyone to get seated. No one noticed the puppy on Sam's lap, well the tiny puppy was entirely covered by his hand. Most of the people spoke tonight, Sam did not. The group has an hour talking then we have snacks together for another hour or more. The talking hour was almost up.

I turned to look at Sam. He had a tear sliding slowly down his cheek. I put my hand on Sam's arm. Are you ok Sam? He slowly turned his head and said; this is the nicest thing anyone has ever done for me. I have a friend now. I tried not to cry. What is your friend's name? I think I will call her Lizzie. By now I was rapidly blinking my eyes. Lizzie is a wonderful name for her. You bring Lizzie next meeting. Sam smiled, I will. He lifted Lizzie to kiss her head. Lula spotted the puppy and that was the end of the talking portion. Everyone gathered around Sam. Sam explained that Lizzie was his new friend. Cole and I got up and he took my hand. A tear spilled out over my cheek, and he handed me a napkin. Ok, I have to get a hold of myself. He whipped out his phone and took a picture of me drying my eyes. What are you doing Cole? We need pictures, and this moment is so I don't know what to call it, but you almost have me crying. Did you hear what he said to me? Yes, and I saw your eyes blinking. Good control there. I really didn't want my make-up running down my face. I have to get some water-proof mascara for our wedding, I have to get that on my list.

We took some snacks and I ate about seven of his cookies. These are really good Cole. Thanks; I brought them for others, but hey eat another half dozen. After people had a chance to hold Lizzie; they made their way to the snack table. One woman who was close to Sam's age, took him by the arm to the snack table for him to try a piece of her cake while she held the puppy.

Cole said in a loud voice; I have an announcement to make. Lisa and I are getting married on Valentine's Day at school and you all are invited. We will get you the invites when they get here.

As we drove home, I looked at Cole. I was so, I don't know what the word it, overwhelmed when Sam said, "I have a friend." It just felt like my heart was ripped apart that he was so lonely. He is not lonely anymore because of you. You brighten his world with a friend and now Lizzie has a home and a friend too.

I got home and the dogs stood looking at me instead of running to the back door. Sorry girls, Lizzie had a higher calling. I had to go out the back door before the dogs would follow me. I emailed my sister about being in the wedding. I told her a pink dress if she had one. I had an email that told me my invitations would be delivered tomorrow and the wedding sign in book the day after. Another email told me that the supplies for the favors would be here Friday.

I texted Cole and asked about gifts for the wedding party, I could get pens for the men with their names and our wedding date engraved, and jewelry boxes for the women with their names. He thought it was perfect. Are you saying I am perfect or what I think of is perfect? Both; he said. Good answer man! I went online and ordered everything from the Things to be Remember site. I would have to go tomorrow and make a deposit. I went to the kitchen and packed up dishes, pans, pots, silverware, glasses, blenders everything. We would be getting everything we needed from the registry and what Cole already had. Wednesday would be a long day. I let the dogs in. We went directly to bed.

We got up early and did a long run. I shower and changed. My hair was growing. It must be the vitamins the OB doctor had given me. The girls had their breakfast and I decided to eat the left-over take-out. I worked on the slide show and added the pictures of Cole and myself. I really had to get more. I took some pictures of the dogs playing tug of war with a long fluffy worm. I added in the pictures of Lizzie too. Then, I looked at the poster boards and I wanted to cry. Nope, I have too much today. I stacked them and put them into bags for carrying. A heavy knock on the door startled me.

It was the men from the women's shelter. I put the dogs outside. Hi guys, thanks for coming. Thank you miss for your donation. Ok, let's get started, the living room furniture, TV, end tables, lamps, the dining room and the bedroom and boxes on the porch from the kitchen. I even had them take stuff from the basement. Everything including seasonal decorations I kept the ornament box but gave away the tree. When it was time for the bedroom, I had them take my bed and furniture. I had to keep Nicole's bed, for the baby. They took it all. I gave them each a hundred dollars and a coke.

I texted Cole and told him that the men had come, now the house felt empty; which it was. The only room not touched was the tiny room with my crafting table. He texted me; do I needed my folding chair. Yes, for when I eat breakfast.

Another knock on the door and I opened it to the Realtor. Hey girl I hear you are getting married. Wow news travels fast. Ok, lets; what happened here, you look like you have already moved out. No, the men from the women's shelter just left and hour ago, I donated all my furniture and TV. I am getting married on Valentine's Day, so it's one less thing to think about. That was so generous of you. You really are a wonderful person. Thank you. After signing forms and picture taking, she left.

I let the dogs in. Hey girls we still have your beds. The dogs walked around the house as if it was the first time, they were in it. I know things are moving fast. We will have a new home to live in and well a new life too. Life is really changing fast. We have each other, oh, really you just think in my sensitive state of mind I should be giving you girls two biscuits each instead of one, right!

I checked the mail, and the invitations and thank you cards had come. I put the mailing labels on the invitations and took them to the post office. The others Cole would put into the teacher's mailboxes. I called Lula and asked if I could drop off the invitations for the group, since she had their address. I dropped off the deposit for the wedding party gifts.

When I got home, I walked through the house. My footsteps echoed. I went upstairs to Nicole's room and lay on her bed with her blankie. The dogs found me and jumped on the bed and curled up.

Lisa, Lisa wake up. The bed was bouncing I opened my eyes and Cole was bent over me. Hey sleepy head. Max was trying to get Cole's attention, and Bella was turning around in endless circles trying to get comfortable. What time is it? It's 5:30. I have been calling and texting you. I came over and knocked but you didn't answer, and the door was unlocked so I came in. I was so tired. I know little mama. You will have plenty of days like that. Can we get tacos? Sure, let's go out. I can't believe how empty your house is. If you want to stay with me, we can move you and pups in. That is sweet. No, we will be fine. I still have to get a wedding dress and you are not supposed to see it. He leaned in and kissed me sweetly. Ok princess let's go eat. Before I forget here are the invitations for the people at school with their names on it. I mailed the ones to our families and friends. This way I can check this off my list.

We sat eating tacos, well lots of tacos to be exact. I don't know why I love tacos so much. I better take the dogs for two long runs tomorrow. You still look sleepy. I feel sleepy. Ok let's get you home and back into bed. You have been doing a lot lately. Slow down, focus on one thing at time. What are you doing tomorrow? I took a picture of all the taco wrappings and Cole. I am working on the slide show I said with my mouth really full. I think I might do one for Nicole's memorial too. Are you going to eat that taco?

Do you want me to come over and make dinner? I gave away my pots and pans. Oh, well I can pick you up and the dogs to come over for dinner. No, we can just meet you, what time would like us to come to Cole's Castle? How about we do 4:30? Since you don't have pots and pans you can come over every night for dinner. Cole you don't have to do that. I am going to be your husband and you are going to make me a father, making dinner, which we both have to eat anyway is a pleasure I want to do for you. It will also help the dogs ease into a new home. So, from today dinner at Cole's Castle forever. He leaned over and kissed me on the nose.

When I got home, I let the dogs out. The house was so empty. I missed everything, maybe I do need to slow down I really should have thought this out. Someone was enjoying my furniture and TV tonight and that was more important. I got ready for bed and let the dogs in. I was so tired, we curled up and slept.

Max woke me licking my face. Good thing you have puppy breath. I let the girls out and had a bowl of cereal. I had kept one of each dish and one pan for my eggs. I had a coffee maker and toaster. I took the girls for a long run that had Max and me panting.

I wondered how Sam was doing with Lizzie. I smiled to myself. When we got home; I changed and looked in the mirror. Hey baby girl things are moving fast. **Mom, getting that puppy for Sam was the sweetest thing ever. Think about the happiness you have given him. Maybe he won't be grumpy anymore. You should slow down some the house is empty and what happens if you get company, they have nowhere to sit! Mom don't keep eating tacos or you will get fat, keep my body healthy for the baby. I know how you love your chocolates, but you need to back off. Don't embarrass me at the memorial with pics of me young and half naked. Be happy mom I love you.** Ok baby girl, I will remove some of the pictures, I love you too.

I worked on the poster boards again. Then made a slide show with music. The wedding sign in book came and I put it into a box. I would show Margaret on Saturday with the wedding planner. I went to the mall to pick up the wedding party gifts. They were so beautiful. No body better back out I thought.

I took the girls for another run, I wanted them to be tired when we went to Cole's Castle. I showered and changed and took some extra time with my make-up and clothes. I wanted Cole to see me at my best not like last night snoring with my mouth open, no doubt. When we got there the driveway was packed with cars. Oh boy what was this. I let the girls out of the car. I got my phone out to text him, but he opened the front door and said come on. As I got closer to him, I asked, what is going on?

My family, well; all of my family is here, and they brought lots of food with them and yes gluten -free. The wanted to congratulate us. When I got home, they were all here. What could I do? Right, surprise! Do I look ok? You look really great. Did you sleep well? Yes, thank you for asking. He kissed my nose and took my arm and lead me into the house.

I knew his whole family even the names of his nieces and nephews. We had been to plenty of barbecues and Christmas parties with his family. The family also knew Nicole as she regularly babysat for Cole and his wife, and for Cole's sister's children. So, why was I so nervous.

No sooner did I take two steps into the house and I was being hugged by his mother. Then the hugs continued from father, sister, brothers, and sister in laws. The kids were more interested in Bella and Max. After an hour, I felt like part of the family. Everyone was so kind. One of Cole's little nieces, who Nicole used to babysit for pulled on my hand. Nicole can you read me a story; I have my book. Long pregnant pause. No one seemed to hear the request, but Cole did. I looked at him terrified for a moment. Focus, one thing at a time. Sure honey, I can read to you. We sat down on the floor. Having a body that's 23 and not 44 I could sit on the floor and actually get up. While I read the story to her, Max came up and started to play with her, she got up and left. Ok, that was close. Cole gave me a look that said that was close.

After more hugs and kisses I took my leave a little early citing the dogs' needs. Cole walked me to my car and opened the door. That was close, but you didn't panic, the look on your face I thought you would, but you kept it together. He kissed me and with the sounds of the kids' voices oohs and yuck!

When we got home the dogs flopped on the floor. Tired, are we? I went to curl up in bed with Nicole's blankie. I had the whole bed to myself, aww.

We all slept in till almost noon. I got up and went downstairs to find Max half way on Bella's back trying to bite her tail. Let's go out. I made the last of the eggs. I had to get more and keep up my skills. I wanted Cole to try my eggs. I heard a truck pull up and looked out to see the UPS guy dropping off a package on my front door. It must the favors. I opened the box and sure enough it was. I decided inside the photo slot on the lid, I would put a poem. Roses are red. Violets are blue. I love you. Forever I do.

I went onto my computer and printed out the poems, 100 of them on pink paper. I would ask Margaret if she would help me cut them out. I packed them in my car along with the sign in book. I took the dogs for a long run. I didn't want to get fat, but I was hungry now all the time, and I knew it would get worse. I wrapped all the wedding party gifts with red heart tags with the poem on it.

Now, I wanted to call my brothers and sister. I called my brothers and linked the calls. Ok my bros I have something very important to ask you. Will you both walk me down the aisle when I get married? I was so happy that they were happy. I knew they were a little offended that they weren't in the wedding party. Now everyone was happy. I texted Cole and Margaret and let them know.

Dinner at Cole's Castle was so good. The girls lay by the fireplace sleeping since I took them for another long run. Cole asked about how the arrangements for the memorial were going. Margaret took care of most of it. I have the revised poster boards, a slide show with music. It's at the funeral home in their large room which can hold about 80 to 90 people, with flat screen TVs on the walls. I just need tables set up along the walls to put the posters on. We will have a chance for people to say something if they wish. I don't know the details but there will be food.

Now, let's talk about what we will wear to the wedding! Should I get a tux? No, only if you want to. No, I don't. I have a really nice black suit. A pink shirt would be perfect. The men can wear red. Ok I will get the guys together on Sunday. I don't know what I should do about the girls. Should I do them all the same or make the all different? Make them different, have fun. Ok, lets text them and we can meet at the mall on Sunday. I know Margaret will want to be in charge.

Cole looked at me and took my hand. Ok, the next item is us. We haven't talked about us intimately. Isn't that something that you don't really talk about but just, I don't know feel your way around. He laughed, you got me there. I mean you being pregnant. We could wait till the baby is born. I smiled, yea we could or not wait that long, let's see how things heat up. I shoved his shoulder and he chuckled. Ok, Lisa you are in the driver's seat for this.

Ok, time to go because tomorrow we meet the Margaret's niece the wedding planner. I had to call dogs twice before them came. It must be nice and toasty by the fireplace. I have all the things in my car I wanted to show Margaret, how about I pick you up at 9:30.

Margaret was there with her niece Wendy, bright and early the next day. Cole and I walked in holding hands carrying our box of favors. She had coffees ready with blueberry muffins. I showed them the favors, Wendy took the box and said we got this. Oh, really, you sure there are hundred and I have more boxes in the car. Wendy was perky, she said she would take the wedding party gifts and the wedding sign in book as well. The only thing you need to do is show up. Wendy pulled out a book. Let's look at Valentine's Day wedding cakes. That's really a thing, Cole asked. Yes, it's one of the most popular days. Cole you pick the cake; the only part I am interested in is the icing on the cake. We all laughed. Cole had good taste. He picked almond cake that had bridges on either side of a four- layer cake with roses and hearts.

Next item Lisa is your head piece. Wendy pulled out a box from under her chair. My aunt told me you weren't doing the traditional wedding dress and had not a lot of hair. She pulled out a wedding hat with short veil. This hat is very comfortable for women who don't have a lot of hair. It covers your head and is made of a cooling material that will keep you comfortable. It had tiny white pearls and iridescent sequins. It is perfect I love it. Margaret grinned, good because I already bought it for you. I am really glad you know my taste. I told you Wendy is good.

We need to pick out your flowers. White tulips and white roses wrapped in sheer red ribbon I said.

Alright, that was easy. We will use the same for the table settings for the wedding party and guests. Next, item is your vows. Are you making them or just the standard vows? Cole and I looked at each other and at the same time said "standard". That was very easy.

How about the photographer. We looked at each other and said Paul at the same time too. Cole explained that Paul was our friend and was given the job. Ok, Wendy said, I will need his number and the numbers to all the people in the wedding party. Margaret stood up and asked Cole to her take the boxes out of my car and put them into her car. I flipped through Cole's phone to get his families' numbers as well.

Wendy, still so chirpy said we will meet up again to make sure we have everything perfect. I will meet you at the mall for the clothes shopping of the wedding party, and we will get Paul to take some pictures. Wow Wendy, you are great. Here, before Margaret comes back. I want to give you these checks. One for the flowers, one for the cake, one for you. Oh, there is no need for you to pay me. This is trial run. Hum, well I am making it for $1000.00. Take these checks and don't tell Margaret. That is way too much money. No, I insist I know you will take all the worry from me and that's worth it.

Also, the rehearsal and dinner we will talk tomorrow, but think about what you might want. Cole and Margaret came back. I eyed them suspiciously. I think they were talking about me, but I couldn't tell.

We left the coffee shop and went looking for wedding bands. We weren't picky people which was really good for both of us. We chose white gold bands with a matching design. I took some more pictures.

We went to lunch and as we sat, I told him my list is almost empty. That's good you only have two things to focus on. Cole, I hope you are ready. I am; he smirked. No, I mean for the pregnancy hormones. Last month I was grief stricken, now I am soaring high as a kite. I just want boring, routine, nothingness for a while. We could go on a honeymoon to somewhere warm and do nothing all day. Humm, sounds good but I would really love to go to Disney. Really, I was thinking about asking you about Disney! It's the happiest place on earth! We act too much like teachers. Ok, when? The day after we get married for a week. We could get couples spa treatments. Ok, I am on it. Don't even think about it or even make a list. I am texting my mother right now about taking care of the pups and the honeymoon. No stress. Mickey here we come!

We went back to my house and let the girls out. How about I take Max for the afternoon and you can do something with Bella. Thanks that would be great. When you are done, come to my house and I will make us dinner.

Bella and I went to the dog park. Then we went to the pet store so she could get groomed. We walked around the pet store so she could pick out her own toy. We went home and went upstairs. We got into Nicole's bed and she laid her head on my tummy. Bella, our life is never going to be the same. We have had so much loss and now so much gain. We napped for an hour and then went to Cole's Castle for dinner.

Cole opened the front door when we got there, and Max bounded out towards Bella. I took Max for a walk on the park path, wow she is a chick magnet. I laughed, yea, they wanted her not you! Cole's Castle had steak with zucchini and sweet potatoes for dinner. I am never giving you up. This is so, good isn't the word, great, I could eat this for breakfast, lunch and dinner every day. What did you do to make this so good? It's the chef in me. I saved a little for the pups, it will help them love being here. Cole got out two bowl and gave each dog some veggies and steak mixed in.

After dinner, I left early because I was getting tired. The pups were tired too. Walking into the empty house was strange. I had so many memories here. I spent 24 years here. When Richard died, I cleaned out so much. Now, with Nicole gone, I again cleaned out so much. It was empty now. Even the pups could sense the new beginnings that were ahead. We went to bed early.

The next day we met at the mall and introduced Wendy to everyone. The men were easy, red shirt, black jacket, and pants. The men decided to go have lunch in the mall and a few beers and watch the game in the tavern. We had all different pink dresses from long too short to frilly. My sister walked with her arm in mine. She asked if I was ready for this? Yes, I need some happiness and Cole is good looking, smart, kind, and he cooks. What more could a woman want? The girls not only picked different styles but also different shades of pink. This would be fun. We finally met up with the men and had lunch.

I looked at Cole, I love having a big family. I do too. Everyone was laughing and joking and really enjoying the day. When we said our good byes to everyone. We picked up pepperoni pizza and ate dinner sitting on the back steps watching the pups tug on a toy in the backyard.

Cole took my hand, and said I know you think about her every day. My tears just spilled down my cheeks. I do miss her, even though I can see her hear her. Sometimes I feel like my heart aches so much it will just burst. Max came over to me with the toy in her mouth. I pulled it and tossed it so Bella could catch it. Nicole would have loved Max. So, you do it for her.

Monday morning came to quick. I was trying to fill out my little booklet which I had been neglecting. I was really trying to honestly fill it out. I would tell Gertrude pregnant hormones made me crazy.

When I sat down in Gertrude's office, we talked about Nicole's memorial in four days. She asked me if I had prepared a speech for that day. I hadn't thought about it. Maybe tell some funny stories, thank everyone for their kindness and support. Lisa be specific, what kindness and what support. Well, for me it means taking the time to send me a card or an email. I didn't feel so alone like the world was going on around me, without me. I felt kindness that some one cared enough to share their feelings with me. I felt supported like I wasn't the only one who was hurt and in pain. Seeing people reaching out their hand or a hug, I am not alone we share the grief together. Gertrude smiled, that's what you say. Since this week is going to be a tough week, we won't do the booklet this week. Remember if you need me, call me.

Now I was feeling down. Debbie Downer brought me down. I stopped at WAWA and got a salad I really wanted to eat healthy, so I also grabbed a Butterfinger. Balance I thought.

When I got to Dr. Light's office, I was told he was out on an emergency and would not be back today. Ok, this day was becoming a real dud. I looked forward to seeing him.

I went home and took a run with the pups. Then I showered and changed. I took out the poster boards and took one last look to make sure everything was perfect then packed them up. I watched the slide show once again. I was ready for the memorial. Could I have closure? No, just blend my life with the baby's life and be happy for the gift that was given me.

At 4:30 we jumped into the car and went to Cole's Castle for dinner. The pups were really loving coming here as he fed them treats and no nos. The fireplace became their new home. I made sure I got plenty of pictures. I told Cole about my day and how I just felt down. He hugged me and didn't let go. You will have days like that, we both have experience in that area. Cole kissed the top of my head. You told me once that when you were feeling sad, you would think about people who were less fortunate than you. That would make you realize you had a lot to be happy for. You are absolutely right. I guess I miss my furniture or rather the homey feel. I am glad I donated it, maybe I should have waited two weeks. Then that would be two weeks someone else who has nothing would have nothing still. You're right. Ok, I made you your summer favorite pecan pie and vanilla ice cream. WHAT!

After three pieces of pie I headed home with the pups. I took the pups for a long walk to clear my head and because I should have only had 1 piece of pie. The other two pieces were really tiny slivers I told myself; to soak up the ice-cream.

The next three days were pretty routine. I took the pups for runs and sometimes twice a day. We would go to Cole's Castle for dinner each night and the pups would sit by the fireplace. My sister came over and spent time helping me clean up the house and pack. Margaret would text me with a thumbs up each day. Wendy, let me know everything was organized from decorations and flowers on the stage to set up and break down in the cafeteria. The rehearsal dinner was set up and everyone had been contacted. She came over Thursday and gave me a box. Inside was a replica of my wedding bouquet. This is for you. It's so beautiful, thank you. I love it. After she left, I felt like crying. No, I have a big day tomorrow and I am celebrating my daughter's life.

The day of the memorial service and my birthday it snowed. I took the pups out for a very long run and then we had breakfast. My car was packed and ready. Cole and Margaret texted Happy Birthdays to me. I went on-line to find many birthday wishes. There were birthday wishes from Greta, Mr. Dupree, Dr. Lambs and Dr. Vinke. They were so kind. I thanked everyone even those on Facebook for my birthday wishes.

I groomed Bella and painted her nails pink. Max got her first bath ever. I was going to bring the pups with me. I didn't know if I was allowed, but I would try. It would be a long day from 2:00 to 7:00 with a light snack at 5:00. Margaret had organized it and said everything was taken care of. I would meet her and Cole there at 1:00 so we could set up the poster boards and slide shows. I wanted the dogs to really be relaxed, so I took them for another long run and came home and showered.

This would be the first time I saw a lot of people I knew. Nicole's friends from school, high school, and college would be there. I was really nervous. I tried to remember what Gertrude had said. I would just hug them and say I miss her too. I wore my matching outfit with scarf. I left enough skin showing around my ears so the scars would be present. That should be enough of a distraction I thought. I had bought waterproof make-up and put it in my purse along with tissues and fake glasses.

I stood in front of the mirror. Well baby girl today we celebrate your life. I redid the pictures and put ones of you and Sam. I am nervous, but you are with me. **Happy Birthday mom! Thanks for using my music playlist for the slides, my friends will recognize the music. The pictures and cards were a great idea mom, and I love that you put so many of them with Sam and me. You caked on the make-up, but I still look good. Use some lip gloss, not lip stick. You are strong mom; you can do it. I would have brought the dogs too, don't let anyone tell you they can't be there. Don't cry and mess up your make-up. I want you to celebrate my life and be happy like it's a party. I love you mom always. Don't eat a lot of cake or you will get fat.** Ok, ok, I love you too always sweetie pie. We all love you and miss you and we cleave to the wonderful memories of you that brighten our hearts. Ok, baby girl here we go. I stared into the mirror for another few minutes. You are with me.

It was still snowing when I got the pups into the car. I brought Bella's bed so they would have a place to lie down. When I got the funeral home Cole and Margaret were already there waiting for me. We unpacked the car and I brought the pups. I gave Cole the flash drive to give to the funeral director, so he could put the slide show on the screens. They had large TV screens in the front and on the sides of the room. Long red clothed tables lined the walls on each side. We put up the poster boards in their stands which took more than a half an hour. Cole took the dogs out to walk them and do their call of nature. When he came back, I put the pups to the side near the front. They were pretty tired, so they just curled together and watched us. Bella was used to going places and staying down, Max I wasn't sure about. This was Nicole's dog and she should be here.

Margaret handed me a pamphlet. It had Nicole's face on the front. This is beautiful I said, thank you so much Margaret. Margaret put her arm around my shoulders. We will greet people from 2:00 to 3:00. Then you can say a few words and others will follow. Around 5:00 or 5:30 if there are a lot of people, we can go downstairs for a light dinner. I thought it was just a light snack. Well, it started out that way, but most of the teachers wanted to bring food, and well the cafeteria ladies made ziti and salad, and some are making desserts, cookies, and someone made your favorite buffalo chicken dip. Wow, that was so wonderfully kind and loving for them to do all that.

I am really hungry, is the buffalo chicken dip here? Cole laughed, it is, and I made it. I will go and get you some. Cole, you are the man. He was back in less than a minute. I almost grabbed the plate from his hand. Sorry, I am really hungry. Margaret laughed, and we know why! This is soooo good Cole, did I tell you that you are my favorite person today? He took the empty plate; do you want more? Maybe, do I have time? Laughing all the way downstairs Cole got more dip and chips. Margaret took a chip with dip, Cole you could open a restaurant and just serve this. Thanks ladies! I know right, I am the luckiest woman alive. Cole took the empty plate and put it in the trash. I hugged Cole then Margaret. Thank you both for everything. I could not make it without you both.

Just then, the first 20 of over 100 people that would come today came in from the snow. The snow was coming down faster. The three of us greeted everyone that came in. Cole whispered, the poster boards with the cards was a nice endearment and they see that their card sent matter to you. Within an hour everyone was there, looking at the slide show or reading the cards. Many of the staff from school were there and friends and our neighbors. Let's get started.

I spoke the speech that I had when I was with Gertrude. It was well received, and I could hear coughing and sniffling. I held out the microphone and Margaret went next and the flow started. The stories were funny, some sad, some on the illegal side, heartwarming, and made people smile and laugh.

Cole was holding my hand. Bella was sleeping but someone had Max. Max was a cuddle. Then to my total amazement Greta walked up. I looked at Cole and said that is Greta from Amsterdam. Oh, my gosh, there is Mr. Dupree. Cole he is the one who got Max. Margaret took my other hand and said, yep we know. You knew they were coming? We wanted it to be a surprise. Well it is! I have missed them both so much. They didn't want to miss the memorial or your birthday.

The dinner was great idea, Nicole's friends were talking to the teachers and friends, hugging and smiles. Greta and Mr. Dupree sat with Cole, Margaret and me. I whispered to Greta, so you came with Mr. Dupree. Yes, we managed to get away for a professional follow-up, I have already seen my sister. We are leaving in a couple of hours from here. No, I mean you came with Mr. Dupree. Oh, well we have become good friends. Is good friends include dinners, quiet walks, etc. It may.

The surprises didn't end there. Cole passed out champagne and we made a toast to Nicole. Margaret came out with a rolling table that held a gluten-free cake with three tiers and four smaller cakes connected. She had sparklers for candles, and everyone sang Happy Birthday. We all had cake, even the pups. Cole took them out for nature and had kibble in his car for them.

Mr. Dupree had a chance to spend time with Max. The goodbyes to Greta and Mr. Dupree were hard. I hugged them both for a long time. Greta you have no idea how special this is for me that you both came. Then we were saying our goodbyes to everyone which took over an hour. Everyone by the end of the evening was smiling and most said that this was the most memorable celebration of life. It was almost 9:00 by the time we left.

Margaret said, Lisa when I go, I want you to do this for me. I will Margaret, maybe we can get more than champagne. You better girl! Ok, you got it. Cole laughed at both of us, I would really like something like this too. I heard some people say this was the happiest memorial they had been to, and memorials should be like this. Everyone was smiling when they left. The young people were talking to the not so young people. Nicole is proud of you! Yea, she would have loved it and the music. I wasn't a fan of the music, but all her friends were.

Ok, let's all go home slowly and carefully. The snow is still coming down, and it's so beautiful. When I got home; I let the dogs in and carried the poster boards in. I went back outside and lay down in the snow and made a snow angel. I got up and made another snow angel. One for Nicole and the other for Sam. I stood there watching the snow falling and thinking about my baby girl and the life she would have had.

I was beyond tired and dropped into bed with my clothes still on.

I woke to hear knocking on the front door. I got up, looked down, and realized I never changed for bed. I went to the front door and opened it. Cole had coffees and cake! He looked at me strangely. Yea, I know I was so tired. Well, I am glad I came. He led me to my folding chair and put the coffee in my hand. I will let the dogs out. By the time he got back I had eaten half the cake and all the icing. You really do like icing! Yes, and this is really good I might add. Are you feeling ok? Yes, I was just tired. I have been really tired lately. When I was pregnant with Nicole, I used to sleep sometimes for 15 hours in a day. Ok, today we meet with Margaret and Wendy.

When I had showered and changed, we headed out to the coffee shop for our meeting. I walked outside to see snow still covered the ground. I stopped in front of the snow angels. Cole smiled, you made them last night, is one for Nicole and one for Sam? Yea.

Cole handed me his coffee and carefully walked on the snow to the heads of the snow angels and drew smiling faces on them. I laughed and handed him back his coffee. We stood there for a few minutes in silence. I turned and kissed him. Thank you for being such a wonderful man. You can thank my mother for that. I will. Last night was I don't know the word, a group hug and fond memories that didn't leave me sad but at peace. He hugged me and then opened the car door for me.

Being a chirpy person must be genetics because there were two chirpy people waiting for us. Oh Lisa, Wendy just showed me a picture of your flowers just beautiful Margaret chirped. Everything from the rehearsal dinner to the completed favors was done. I have gotten back all the replies, so everybody is coming. Wendy chimed in, no problem we set aside a few extra for any last minute add on. Rehearsal dinner is in three days. We will get pictures, also the day of the wedding he will be over to take pictures of you and the other girls getting ready. Your DJ said he has all the music, he checked in with Cole. FYI the mayor is wearing his Valentine's day marrying suit. Lisa you will love the decorations on the stage they are so, well you. Oh boy Margaret, I can't wait, I laughed. You will see them at the rehearsal. Cole and I looked at each other and smiled with a quick kiss.

Ok, we will leave these two love birds alone. Wendy and Margaret got up to leave. Lisa I will call you tomorrow Margaret said. Alright, let me know if you think of anything we still need to do. Yes, your dress we can go Sunday and or Monday dearie.

After they left; we sat and looked over my list, everything was checked off except one. What is that at the bottom of your list, Cole asked? Oh, I was just drawing. I would like to get a grave stone and bury Nicole's ashes. Wow, that was a change in subject. I know I caught you off guard. I was thinking of one with a snow angel. We can go look now. I have my plot at the graveyard. I want to use it and put her stone there; next to her dad. Let's go then.

We went to look at headstones. Lots of choices. Howard who owned the placed came out. Mrs. Goodwin, how are you? Well, if I am here, a good chance not where I would want to be. Good point. How can I be of service to you today? Howard, I have my daughter's ashes and I want to bury them next to my husband and have a grave stone. Oh, I am so sorry for your loss. Thank you. I wrote down what I want on it, and could you do at the top a snow angel? Absolutely! You pick which grave stone you want, then come in and look at the photo book to choose which angel you want. We walked around the various head stones holding hands. We came to one at the end of the path. We turned and looked at each other and smiled. Yep, that's the one. We went back down the path and into Howard's office.

That was quick. We want the one at the end of the path. Oh, yes that is a nice one. Here look at some of these photos of angels. If you don't like any of them let me know we can draw one up that you want. After about three quarters of an hour we chose the snow angel we wanted. It will take a few weeks; I will call you when it's done. I am very sorry for your loss.

When we left, we headed to my house to pick up the pups. Hey Lisa, do you think we should have Howard put a smiley face on it. Humm I will have to think about that one.

We went back to Cole's and walked the pups along the park path. Wow this is moving so fast. I am so very happy Wendy is handling everything. It takes such a load off my mind. Good it gives you more time to think about me and our castle. I want to add onto the house in the back and make a large bedroom and family room. The bedrooms are a good size, but a large master bedroom with bathroom. A family room with one wall glass so we can see the park. Also, we can put up an invisible fence for the pups. Great idea, and I will train both to go potty in the back corner of the yard. Bella won't wander off and I think Max will stay near her. After dinner Cole dropped us off. I will see you Sunday night for dinner. Ok, great.

Sunday morning, Margaret was banging on my front door. Really girl! Yes, let's get your dress. Don't forget your veil. We went to a thousand shops; my legs were holding on by bare ligaments. Finally, we found a white dress with a sheer red overlay. The sweetheart neckline had pearls sewn in and matched the veil perfectly. The sleeves were three quarter and a fitted waist. A slim dark red petticoat completed the dress. It was feminine, romantic, and beautiful. We stopped for coffee and a rest. Margaret, I can't go on, we only need shoes now; white sling-back shoes, I will only try on one pair. Let's go to Macy's and get the Chanel sling backs. I am done for the day!

As we walked, I told her about how I needed her help for Cole's wedding gift. I have already picked out the car he wants. What, you are getting him a car! Will you marry me! We laughed heartily. I need you to decorate it and drive it to the school. We need to get Mike, his best man, to drive him to school. I will go tomorrow to the dealership and get all the paperwork done. I will pick you up at home after school, so we can go to the dealership and you drive the car to your place.

So, Margaret do you know what Cole is getting me for a wedding present? I eyed her suspiciously. Really do you think he would tell me. He knows I would tell you in a heartbeat. Any news on your honeymoon? Cole told me not to make a list or worry, we are going to Disney. You two act more like kids then grown-ups. Don't most teachers act like kids?

After Margaret dropped me off, I hung up my wedding dress. Let the pups out, because I was not capable of doing anymore walking. We went to Cole's Castle for Shepherd's Pie. I had to sit with my feet on a chair because they hurt so bad. Cole rubbed my feet till I fell asleep in the chair. He woke me at eight with some hot coco and flavored marshmallows. You are a wonderful man! I put some little mini marshmallow in there for baby. I laughed as I pushed around the marshmallows with my finger. Ok, we need to get home. Cole helped me up out of the chair. The pups didn't seem to notice. They really like it here. Dinner tomorrow let's do 5:30 I have to pick up a few things. Ok, I said sleepily.

I did not want to get up this early, but Max's tongue was touching my nose and I couldn't take it. Ok, wearily I got up and let the pups out then made breakfast. I sat looking into my coffee cup. I was going to get married the day after tomorrow. Everything in the past two months have drained my brain. I felt like I couldn't think intelligently, but instant at the now moment just enough to move on to the next minute of life.

We went for a 2-mile run. I needed to make sure I didn't gain to much weight. I was only two months pregnant and had gained two pounds. Considering how much I ate and slept lately, that was pretty good.

Monday morning, I went to see Gertrude. She was actually smiling when I went through the door. I hear your daughter's memorial was an uplifting beautiful event. Oh, it was, and having your sister there made it special. Did you meet her friend Mr. Dupree? We didn't talk too much about me, but we did go into overtime again. I told her I wouldn't see as I was going to be on my honeymoon. Before I opened the door to leave, I turned and hugged her and said thanks. I could see it really matter to her. I didn't see a ring on her finger. Maybe she should get a puppy; I thought.

Next stop, WAWA then to Dr. Light's office. The store was crowded so I couldn't get something healthy, so I opted for water, Butterfinger, and M&Ms. Since I didn't see Dr. Light on my last Monday, I hoped all was well with him.

I went up to his office and knocked on the door. He called, come in Lisa. He was conferencing on the screen with Dr. Lambs. Lisa come sit. Hi Dr. Lambs. Lisa, we were discussing your OB-GYN and contacted him, so he doesn't put you through extensive testing. With your consent he will be keeping us updated on your progress. We have discussed how your file will be kept separate in his office locked up and labeled with YU instead of your name. We also have a name of a dentist who we have worked with and will be discreet and will forwarded us information on your health. After blood tests were taken; I let Dr. Light know I wouldn't see him next Monday. I said my good byes and headed home.

I packed my bag for our honeymoon. Since most of the clothes and shoes I had were for winter, I only packed a few. I could get some clothes when we were on our honeymoon. I couldn't get it out of my head. I was now 45 going on a honeymoon. This is weird, I should write a book, but I don't think anyone would believe it. I cleaned up the house, which wasn't a lot since there was not much to clean. I packed up crafting room for moving.

I called the bank to let them know I was buying a car and was going to write a check. I called the dealership and told them I was coming in later today, and which cars I wanted to see. I went online to update my Facebook and return comments. So many had pictures posted from Nicole's memorial and many wonderful and positive comments. It warmed my heart.

Picking the car, I would give Cole as a wedding present was easier than filling out the paper work. I called Margaret to let her know I was at the dealership. She said Mike would drop her off so we wouldn't have to go back and forth. She said Mike had some ideas about decorating it. Oh boy, I thought Mike is a little crazy I hope he doesn't use his signature toilet paper! When they got there, they both approved of my choice. Margaret drove the car to her place so she could bring it to the school in two days.

I ran home to pick-up the pups and off we went for dinner at Cole's castle. When I got to Cole's house it seem deserted as the lights were out. His car was there. The pups jumped out of the car and Max started barking. Hey, Max it's ok. I think; as we walked up to the house, Max was still barking which was making me nervous. I knocked on the door and it flew open. SURPRISE! It was. There must have been close to 50 women in his house, including my sister, his mother, his sister, friends, other teachers, and Margaret of course. Cole looked at me and said, I didn't have choice, I did make you buffalo chicken dip. Well, then that makes everything better, I laughed, and he kissed me. I am out of here, this is women only, and with his jacket he left.

Max stopped barking and was being passed around. Bella went over by the fireplace to lie down. Margaret came over and said, ok doll, let's get started on your hat, and she tied a paper plate to my head. Let the fun begin. The bridal shower was a success and we received everything on our registry. Margaret sat next to me to finish the bows on my hat. We thought having it here, you wouldn't have to pack it in the car and bring it here, we saved you a step. Thank you, but how did Cole take it? Well his eyes did get really big and I thought he was going to say no, but then he laughed. It was a surprise, the lights out I thought something was wrong, especially since Max was barking. This is great, Margaret, everyone should have a friend like you.

After all the cleaning up, saying good byes, Cole came home. Margaret said, oh Cole's here, I will take my leave, so you too love birds and settle your nest. Cole, come look at the fully appliance stocked kitchen! Cole patted both pups before coming into the kitchen. I had all the cabinets opened so he could see we had all new dishes, cooking utensils of varying sorts, deluxe coffee maker, silverware, crockpot, toaster, toaster oven, mixer, blender, steamers, pots, pans, and knives of chef quality. WOW good grief Charlie Brown; this must be a dream. We also have got the bedding, blankets, towels and table settings. He put his arms around my waist and lifted me around in a circle. Cole's castle is ready for its' queen. I laughed and kissed him on his forehead. I will love the meals you make! Oh sure, didn't we discuss this, am I doing all the cooking? Well, I can pour cereal for breakfast and make sandwiches for lunch. Ok I can live with that. After sitting on the couch and talking about the days past and upcoming, Max jumped up on the couch and lay her head on Cole's lap and drifted off to sleep. We all fell asleep and didn't wake till six the next morning. Cole's alarm clock in the bed room went off and he quietly got up leaving me and the pups to continue sleeping.

Cole left a note on the kitchen table, saying he loved us, he drew paw prints, and would see us tonight so we could go to the rehearsal dinner together.

I woke about nine, and the pups were still sleeping. Wow this is going to be my new home, it was so cozy, new smell, matching, which I never had. I got the dogs up and we went home to have breakfast and take a 2-mile run. When we got back, I showered and changed.

I have everything ready for tomorrow, but what about pictures. My house is empty. How could we get the pictures of wedding party getting ready with no furniture in my house? No one would have a place to sit. I texted Margaret even though she was at school and asked if we could get ready at her house about noon for pictures and such. The text came back immediately, yes; I was planning on it. Ok, her and Wendy have it all under control. Focus, Wendy and Margaret have it all under control.

Since I had a few hours before meeting Cole for the dinner, I decided to get my toes and nails done in a French tip with a rich color red. I also shopped for red lacy underclothes for under my wedding dress, and something to well you know, sleep in. I got home and let the pups out. It was time to go the Cole's, we would then meet everyone at the school at four thirty for practice, then have dinner.

Cole and I got to the school and went into the lobby. Everyone was there, from my brothers, sister, his parents, brothers, sister, Wendy and the mayor. We went into the auditorium. It was amazing, an arch was on the stage covered in white roses with red hearts with sheer red ribbon. Hanging from the ceiling were iridescent glitter hearts of varying sizes with red and white balloons. A long red runner down the aisle and heart and flower arrangements attached to the ends of seats. This is wonderful thank so much everyone. We had to do three trial runs, as my brothers kept stepping on my feet.

The dinner was great. Everyone was enjoying themselves and the wine flowed freely, and I do mean freely, till some of the laughter was a little too loud. Wendy and I went over the last of the details and would see each other tomorrow around noon. Dinner lasted almost three hours, and everyone started to take their leave. Our families are already family. Cole kissed me on my nose as we left.

When we got to Cole's he asked me to come in for a few minutes. I sat down on the couch and Cole came out of the bedroom with a red box. He handed me the box and said I love you and I wanted to give you your wedding present, but you can't open it until tomorrow morning. Oh, Cole, can I open it? Nope, not until tomorrow. So, I could technically open it at midnight. He laughed, yea I suppose you could. I am feeling really excited now that tomorrow is the big day. It feels like it was supposed to happen between us, since we have known each so long. It feels Wright, Mr. Wright! Yes, it does and even though it was quick, it feels like a long time. He wrapped his arms around me, ok little mama and kissed me gently on the lips. I better get home and get some sleep. Good night Mrs. to be Wright. Good night Mr. Wright.

When I got home, I let the pups out, and stared at the box, no, I couldn't be dishonest the day before we got married. I could shake it and guess. I shook it gently next to my ear. It just rattled with tissue paper. I could stay up until midnight! Oh, darn, I really wanted to open it. I have been known to rewrap Christmas presents for many years. Ok pups, tomorrow I will be Mrs. Wright, and you too will have new last names and need dog tags with your new address.

We all plopped into bed. Oh, pups this is our last night together. I got my phone out. Ok Max let's play peek-a-boo. Max in her little girly voice said, "What do you call a dog that meditates? Why aware wolf!" Max waved good bye. I didn't want to check on the other video hits, but Max looked sad. Max, some of these have over 8,000 hits and the first few have over 42,000 hits. I have to show this to Cole. I sent him a text. I had to send one to Margaret. She answered right away. Are you ready for tomorrow? No, I changed my mind. The phone rang within seconds. Hi Margaret, I was just kidding, I wanted to see how long it would take you call. I told her about my red box that Cole gave and how I couldn't open it until tomorrow. We talked for another hour about our lives and how they keep changing. Finally, I said good night.

I was so tired; but does anyone ever sleep the night before getting married. Yes, if you are pregnant you sleep a lot. We got up late and I took the pups for run. The weather was nice and brisk. As I was making breakfast for the last time as a single woman and pregnant one now; the phone rang.

Good morning Lisa, I just want to call speak with you for a few minutes. Sure, Mrs. Wright. You can call me mom from now on. I'd like that, mom. I just wanted you to know how over joyed we are that you are part of our family. I am so happy to see Cole smile and laugh again, it's been way to long and it's because of you that our son is happy again. Tears were welling in my eyes and I had to clear my throat. Cole is the most wonderful, caring, kind hearted man and it's because of you, thank you for making such a loving son and husband; mom. I could hear the shakiness in her voice. I am so happy you will be taking care of my son. I sniffed and said, I am so glad I don't have my make up on right now. We both laughed. She told me how her and Margaret were going to take care of the pups while we were on our honeymoon. Thanks mom, for calling, it really made my day fill up with joy and love.

As I hung up the phone, I cried happy tears. I have a mom again and she was a loving, caring, and great mom. I wonder how she is going react when she finds out I am pregnant. Should we tell her. No, I didn't want her to think I married Cole because I was pregnant, or vice versa. Could we pull off that baby came a month and half early? We had plenty of time to think about that issue.

I stood in front of the mirror. Well baby girl, we are getting married today. I went and got the red box and stood in front of the mirror again. What do you suppose this is? I opened the box to find the most beautiful strand of pearls with earrings and bracelet. I don't know how he paid for them, but these were mighty expensive, like three or four months of paychecks. His mom and dad must have helped him, maybe that's why she called, she knew I would open them today. She wanted me to know we are a family. What do you think? **Mom, they are very beautiful, just like you, or me. You are making a family with my baby and I am really happy and want you to be really happy with Cole. Have fun, enjoy this day and everyday forward. Happy wife means happy life. I love you mom, just be happy today and every tomorrow.** Thanks baby girl. It's time to get ready.

I showered and changed into casual clothes. I have to put my make-up on now because if they see me without make-up I will look exactly like Nicole. Which I do. So, I took a lot of time to put on my make-up. No one better make me cry. I packed up the car with my suitcase, wedding veil, dress, and red box. I played with the pups and fed them. They were going to have changes in their lives too. I was running late but made it to Margaret's by 12:30.

All the girls were there, Wendy, and Paul taking pictures. We got dressed and posed for pictures like putting on my new pearl necklace which everyone was in awe. Paul took pictures of us doing our hair, drinking, laughing, goofing off and serious pictures with my flowers, looking out a window. My sister sat next to me on the bed and handed me a blue lace garter. This is for you and for something borrowed, and I do want it back, a pinky ring my father had given our mother. She hugged me for a long time and said; you deserve to be happy and stay happy. I told her about Cole's mother calling me and asking me to call her mom. That's the best part of getting married you get more family, my sister hugged me again.

Nobody ever mentioned me having kids I thought. I think because I am 45 years old, they don't want to broach the subject. Too old to have a baby. That's what was missing in the conversations and joking. Little did they know, there was a bun in the oven.

I found a quiet room, the bathroom, and called Cole. Cole the pearls are so incredibly beautiful if we weren't getting married today, I couldn't have accepted them if we were dating. Well, then I guess it's a good thing we are getting married today. Are you nervous? Yea, my mouth is so dry I have been eating Tic Tac breath mints all afternoon. I have some news for you Mrs. to be Wright. Ok, I am listening. After the reception we are heading out to the airport to fly to Florida about 11:00 tonight. We will be picked up at the airport and taken to the honeymoon suite. Then six days of adventure. We have special passes and no waiting time in lines. My mom also has us booked for dinners each night at different parks. Oh, I can't wait this is going to be so much fun. You sound like a little girl. I laughed and thought, I am. By the way we are sending Paul over to take pictures of you guys. I am afraid to look at some of the pictures he took, because my sister and Margaret have been drinking a lot. Ok, I will see you walking down the aisle at 4:00 today Mrs. to be Wright. Ok then, Mr. Wright it's a date.

I hung up the phone and looked in the mirror. Now, I am getting nervous. Baby girl I love you so much and wish things could be different, but I guess they are the way they; are because of you. **Mom stop getting emotional, you will start crying and mess up your make-up which looks really awesome by the way. I wish you had more time to plan the wedding. Then you could have planned a cool dance moves when the bride and groom dance and shock everybody. Or you could have gotten Wedding Crashers, that would be hysterical. Really cool, have Max jump out of the wedding cake. Stop being nervous you have done this before. It's the best day ever, Mom, so snap out of it and enjoy and remember I love you Mom to the moon and back.** I love you too even more baby girl.

When I came out of the bathroom everyone was staring at me. What! I wanted to call Cole. There was a loud resounding sign of relief in the room. We thought you fell in or got lost. I am here and who has the Tic Tac mints?

When it was time, late, well fashionably late we set off for the school. We were laughing and joking. Who gets married at a school? It was kinda funny getting married where you work. The parking lot was packed. Ok girls, now I am getting really nervous. We went into the side door and to the front of the auditorium and outside the doors my brothers and Cole's brothers were waiting. The wedding march started. I hugged my brothers and said here we go. The wedding party started down we waited a couple beats and my brothers arm in arm walked me down the aisle. I was happy, I had lost a lot, and now gained a lot. I may never know why things happen, but I want to always have them make me a better person. I was getting a great guy. My eyes were glued to Cole. He looked really, and I do mean really, great in a suit.

The ceremony lasted 15 minutes and we kissed to a thunderous applause. We walked down the aisle together and stood at the doors to greet everyone. There were lots of hugs and kisses. The principal laughed and said this could start a trend. Sam came with the woman from our grief group and had Lizzie in his pocket with her head sticking out. Shh Lizzie didn't want to stay home alone. Mums the word, I laughed. Everyone finally into the cafeteria and we posed for pictures with family and wedding group.

Charlie announced the wedding group as they entered the cafeteria and then Mr. and Mrs. Cole Wright. We had our groom and bride dance to *Somewhere* then Cole with his mother danced. We sat at the head table and there were the wedding gifts for each of the wedding party. What a good idea. The table cloth had thousands of tiny heart confetti all over and I do mean all over; thanks Margaret.

The present table had 20 to 30 gifts and a Valentine Day's box filled with cards. The tables were called, and everyone had to get up and walk the cafeteria food line. That is good, I love seeing grown-ups in the food line. Mike gave a simple funny toast that had us all roaring with laughter. He should be a stand-up. The music and dancing were fun and funny. We hadn't talked about the cake smashing. I looked at Cole and said, I really don't want cake in the face since we are leaving right from here is that ok with you? Well, as long as when we eat our first anniversary cake, I get to do a face smash, I can wait. Deal.

Where is Margaret? Cole said, she went to let the dogs out and bring them to my house. Her and my mom will be taking care of them and it's right next to the park path. Mike said he would drive us to the airport. Oh, he did, did he! I bent forward to look at Mike, who grinned and said, "At your service love birds.". When we finished eating, we went around to all the tables. I poked Cole, isn't it funny seeing all these adults sitting at kid sized cafeteria tables. He looked around the room and we both laughed. I will not see this room in the same light again. We did the garter thing and bouquet toss. Wendy caught the bouquet and a young new teacher caught the garter. Humm I think they make a great pair, and so did everyone else. We cut the cake and fed each other over the deafening chants of smash it and cake face.

 The evening was filled with love, good friends, and caring family. It was time to start our honeymoon and new adventure. We said our good byes and hugs and kisses. Everyone lined up outside with rice and cameras. When we got outside and saw the car decorated with tin cans in the back. Mike had put pink tulle from the hood ornament to each side view mirror with cut out hearts and a three -foot- long flower arrangement on the grill. Pink, white, and red heart shaped balloons on all the door handles. Whoa we are driving in that. Where did he get that car from? Happy Wedding day Cole, that is your new car, it's my wedding gift to you. WHAT! That is the car I have been looking at for a year now. He picked me up and twirled me around and kissed me. You are the best wife ever. Yea, I think so. We ran with our heads bent so we wouldn't get rice in our faces into the backseat of the car. Mike was behind the wheel. He turned and smiled, like the new cruise machine. I will take good care of it while you are gone, ha ha ha. You better Mike, because I know where you live.

Cole ran his hands over the seats and sniffed. I love the color, smell, and you. Thanks, were you talking about my color and smell? The ride to the airport was short. Our luggage was in the trunk. Cole took a while to admire the tires, trunk, dashboard, engine all the bells and whistles. Finally, we headed to the ticket counter with people staring at us. When a woman stopped and said, "Congratulations", I realized we still had our wedding clothes on. We looked at each other and laughed. Maybe we should have changed.

We checked in along with our luggage. I have my head scarf, but it doesn't match my dress can we look in some of the shops. After three shops we found a white head scarf and I went into the bathroom to put it on. Are you thirsty? Yes. We got some bottled water and sat by the windows watching the planes come in and out. It started snowing.

Cole took my hand and said in the cheeriest voice he could muster, how about finding some hot sunny clothes for Florida? He pulled me up and when I looked into his eyes, I could see the concern. I knew he was doing this for me. Well, let's look for some racy speedo bathing suit for you. Only if you wear one too. And we found some really racy bathing suits. I was reluctant, but Cole convinced me we would never see these people again, I relented.

We heard the call for boarding and rushed to the gate. His mother had gotten us first class so, we went in right away. Cole kept talking to me and asking me questions so I wouldn't look out the windows. We had large lounge chairs and put our feet up. I am tired it's been a long day and baby mama wants a nap. Yes, get some sleep I will wake you when we get there.

I closed my eyes because I was so tired. I was also very nervous and didn't want to ruin Cole's honeymoon with my stress. I felt I had a right to be stressed and with just cause. I fell asleep within minutes. Lisa wake up we are here. I woke with a start. Oh, that was quick, feeling awkward I got up. We were the first to leave the plane. Did I snore at all? No, do you usually? A little.

Our honeymoon was everything a honeymoon should be and then some. We laughed, swam, screamed on rides, watched fireworks, had romantic dinners, and a really cool spa tub in our room. We got pictures will all the characters which was no small feat it took the concierge some phone calls to make it happen. We got our passport stamped in each country and took boat, bus, and safari tours. I was sad when we had to pack to go home. Let's live here, we could become characters and work here. I would be Belle and you could be the Beast. I am not so sure I want to be a Beast; some kids were scared of him and ran. We will come back when the baby is about four or five and we can do this all over again. Yes!

Coming home to my new Cole's Castle was a little strange, but when I saw the pups bound out of the house to greet us, I knew this was my home now. Cole hugged his mom and thanked her. The dogs were both on top of me licking me in the face yuk. Come on girls, Cole picked up Max, wow you are so big what happened mom have you been feeding her spinach. Margaret came out of the house and pulled me up. The cutie puppies were so good, not one accident. Margaret and his mom discreetly left as this was the first time as a married couple, we would enter this home. We waved good bye and Cole lifted me up and carried me into the house. Welcome home Mrs. Wright.

The house smelled like vanilla almond. In the corner were presents stacked in rows. It's like Christmas. We unpacked and took the pups for a long run. When we came back; we started completing the thank you notes. Since I already had mailing labels, we personally thanked everyone for the gift they gave. The gifts were house décor, bedding, towels, a vacuum with carpet steamer and pet hair attachment, beautiful seasonal table settings for different holidays that matched our kitchen. Margaret must have had a hand in it.

We finally washed and put everything away. Good thing I have that outdoor garage. We will make up some plans for expanding with an indoor closet to store everything. How about we do take out tonight. Tomorrow I am back to work. Let's make a list of food and I will go shopping tomorrow and have everything ready for you to cook dinner. Ha ha, Cole chuckled. We sat and made our first shopping list together.

A few days later the realtor called and said she had sold my house and got $65,000 over what I was willing to sell for. I told her that was great, and I would pay for the closing costs, new owners had enough to pay for. How long before settlement? In two weeks if that is ok with me. They saw that all the furniture was gone, and I told them you just got married, and they want to move in right away. Ok then, that's great I will move the rest of my things out this week. I couldn't wait for Cole to get home to tell him.

When Cole got home from school, I greeted him at the door with the pups jumping all over him. Guess what? What. No, I said guess what. Oh, I don't know, we won the lottery. You are close. What! I sold my house which is paid off for a total of $310,000 dollars. Whoa, are you kidding me? Nope, we can put most of it in our pension plan, so we don't have to pay taxes on it. We have the money to make the additions to the house. You are a great wife. Thanks, I think so too.

Over the weekend we packed up what was left in the house. When I packed the form boards up, I asked Cole if we could bury them with the head stone. He thought it was a great idea. We put the boxes in our outdoor garage. The only thing left was Nicole's and I wanted to save her bedroom set. Thank goodness I had given away all the clothes and furniture before-hand. We had already moved the doggie stuff and it was already clean.

The following Saturday I met with Margaret at the coffee shop our usual spot. How is life treating you Mrs. Wright? Well, I had to change my regular doctors' appointments to once a month since I am going back to work in a few weeks. Cole and the pups all have a schedule, we get really excited when he comes home. We are so compatible, and it feels like it's been a long time. I am really happy. Baby is getting bigger. I will get the ultra sound again this Monday. But I told Dr. Light I want to be surprised. Do you think it's a boy or a girl? I feel like it's a girl. Then since you have insider information, we now know it's a girl. Well, Lisa I have to go and pick up some things so I will see you tomorrow. Tomorrow, what are we doing tomorrow? Oh, sorry I meant I will call you tomorrow. She hurriedly left. Ok then; I thought. What is going on tomorrow?

Cole served me breakfast in bed the next day. Humm it's not my birthday what could be going on! Cole kissed my forehead and said, let's go for a drive in my new car, you know Sunday drive and we could have brunch. Sure, I said looking at him for any hint of what was going on.

As we sat in his new car and drove, I asked so where are we going? Oh, just a drive. So, are you excited about going back to school in a few weeks? Yes, I am a little nervous, I am wondering if any of the kids will jump up and say you are a fraud; you're not Mrs. Goodwin. We showed the students some pictures of the wedding and explained why you were wearing a hat and that you would have a head scarf on. None of the students said anything about you not looking like you. It's been three and half months since you saw them. You are right Mr. Wright. Focus on one thing at a time.

We pulled into the grave yard, and then I remembered about the grave stone. We were silent as we walked up to where my husband was buried. There was the new head stone with the snow angel. The ground us dug up and the poster boards and urn were inside. Margaret walked up behind me with red roses. I hugged her. Thanks this means a lot. We talked and said happy and sad things then tossed in a rose. When we were done, I asked if I could have a few moments.

Oh, my little baby girl. This is so odd; I don't know how to feel. Your body is growing a new life, and your spirit is free. I can see you and hear your voice. That has to be enough for me. You gave me the gift of life and another gift of life to raise. Most people in that crash don't have what I have. I had so much taken and was given much. I miss your little smirk and the way you would hug me tight and finish all my sentences. I have so much and yet sometimes I feel empty. I will do my best for my new husband and your baby. I wept for a long time. **Mom really get a grip; this isn't the first time I have had to tell you this. It is what it is. Live my life to the highest point you can. Have fun, drink-after the baby is born, be your own silly self. I am always with you mom and my heart beats life into you and my baby. Make it a happy life, move on. I will let you know when you are doing something wrong like spoiling my baby and make them become a brat. Max and Bella both need more cuddle time too. You are my mom and I love you unconditionally. So, lets pull it together and go to lunch; pizza would be good.** I know baby girl you are right; I love you so much. Pizza it is. Love you to the moon and back.

The three of us had, strangely enough, pizza. We enjoyed the rest of the day catching a movie and having a light dinner. Margaret finally said good night. We went home and took the pups out for run, which I was in the lead all the way.

The sale of the house brought a wonderful wind fall and we added to our pensions and drew up the plans for home improvement. The plans which Cole's brother and my brother and 8 of their employees would build. We added a large master bedroom with bath room that had a spa tub in front of bay window, facing the woods, two more rooms for a study or craft room. Cole went a little crazy and put a multi-tiered deck with build in benches, flower boxes, fire pit, a wall fountain, and barbecue. I added the treehouse in a low-lying tree with windows. The men said it would be done in time for summer. Cole kept busy with paperwork and permits.

The next few weeks I prepared myself to go back to school for another two and half months. I decided to dye my hair using Paul Mitchel 6C, which I normally used, so I would have something that looked like me. I put in all my retirement paper work. I would finish this school year and retire. With the baby coming I wanted to stay at home. With the money already in my bank account from the airlines, and money from the sale of the house I would stay home and be a full-time mom. I was actually nervous.

I contacted my substitute teacher and we talked at length about what they learned and who liked who and who was being a little harder to handle. She told me about how the kids reacted when they found out that I had been in a plane crash. She took my daughter's picture off my desk and put it in the drawer. Some of the kids really took it hard and the principal gave us some extra counselors to spend time with the kids. The kids were so happy to read your emails and went over the moon when they saw the videos of Max. Cole brought in some of the wedding pictures and the kids were so excited. They are looking so forward to seeing you again.

I was only a little over three months pregnant and wasn't showing other than my boobs were over flowing my bra. My outfits I got for school were mostly dresses and I could hide behind them for a few more months. Up till now I gained 4 pounds and didn't look pregnant. Cole and I hadn't yet decided when to tell anyone that I was pregnant. Margaret told us we should do it soon. She was right, we decided to after I returned to school.

Cole and I drove to school together on April 1st. I was ready to finish the school year. When I walked the halls, it felt so sad that I would only be here for a few more months. I sat behind my desk and enjoyed the quiet. Soon students started trickling in and the hugs and gifts were so touching I couldn't help cry. Which made them cry. We spent the first two hours of our day talking about me and they wanted to hear about the plane crash, the food and people in Amsterdam, famous Facebook Max, wanted to see my hair. I am so glad I did dye my hair. Most of the students thought I looked cool with the short hair, like a bad teacher nobody would mess with.

I was so tired of talking. I had my students each come to the front of the room and tell me what they learned since I was gone and what they are still having a hard time with. When they all finished it was lunch time. After recess we came in and I had the students sit on the floor. Ok, this is my first day back and you all have told me what you are struggling with. I have made 4 groups based on the things you need help with. I have put two experts in your group to help you. Let's do 15 minutes of learning, then we will switch groups again for another 15 minutes.

While I was completing paperwork and the students were in their groups. Ike came up to me and leaned against my desk. He looked at me so sad. What is it Ike? I am so happy you are back. You don't look happy. Maybe you were overwhelmed by it and now that I am here you are so happy you feel like crying in relief or happiness. That's it I feel like crying. It's ok, let's go out into the hallway. I had plenty of tissues in my pocket. Ike hugged me and cried. Feel better, I asked wiping away his tears. Yea, I am happy crying. I know I do that too. Everyone was so busy talking in their groups they hadn't noticed we had left and came back.

The end of the day the students got on their buses and I sat in my room so tired I wanted to put my head down and sleep. My eye lids were actually fluttering. Cole came in and in his loud happy manly voice said how was your first day back?

I looked at him and smiled, I just want to go home and sleep. I am so physically and mentally tired. Ok, let's go and he pulled me up out of my chair. We are having eggs and toast for dinner. Cole had to wake me to get out of the car once we got home. He opened the door and the pups were so really excited to see us. I plopped down on the couch and fell asleep.

Lisa, wake up. Cole's face was up close and personal along with a plate of eggs and toast with bacon. I shifted myself upright and took the plate. I ate slowly and Cole told me how he took the dogs out for a run then showered and changed and then made dinner. After I finished eating Cole took the plate from me and tipped my face upward to face him. Are you ok, where you this tired at school? No,

I was fine at school, I think I told you before, when I was pregnant with Nicole, I slept a lot in the first trimester, and today was exhausting mentally with excitement and nervousness. He carried me to bed, and I slept until morning.

I got up early took the dogs for a run then showered and changed for day two of school. Today we would get back onto our regular schedule. I brought coffee to Cole since he was still in bed. Hey sleepy head time to get up. He opened one eye and said, really! I laughed and ripped the covers off him in a quick swoop. NO, really, the king is wanting just ten more minutes of sleep. Sorry, the birds are singing do you hear them.

We told everyone at school that I was pregnant, which is why I was retiring at the end of the school year. Everyone was so happy for us. Cole's mother was just well, over joyed, as was his father. Our brothers and sisters were so supportive with advice and hand-me-downs.

In May the college called me and asked about my daughter's degree. I told them I wanted to walk in her place. They sent me special invitations, cap, and gown. Cole and Margaret wanted to go with me. I called Nicole's friend Crystal who was so happy to hear I would be joining her. She said that Sam had a brother who was going to walk in his place. We had to take a day off from school for the graduation.

Nicole had worked so hard for her Masters 'degree and I wanted to see her name on it. I tried my best not to cry. It was a very special day.

The next month of school went by quickly. My students were going to the middle school and most cried the last day of school. I gave away almost everything in my classroom, as I really didn't want to take anything home. The students were grateful and helped me pack what I wanted.

The last day of school was also the retirement dinner for the teachers that retired that year. There was only me and Mr. James. I think it should be called a roast as that is really what happened. Teachers made up silly songs, skits, funny jokes, show embarrassing old photos. It was a memorable night. I was sad to be leaving but knew being home with baby was much more important and it's what Nicole would have wanted.

My life had changed so much in a year and half. I was married with a daughter in college and Bella with retirement in the future. I lost my husband of 24 years, lost my precious daughter's spirit, lost my whole body, sold my house. Now, I had Max, a new husband, a new body, a new house, a baby on the way, no job due to retirement, a new family, Dr. Light, Gertrude, a happier grief group. To live life; there is change as the seasons.

True to their word, they finished our home addition, multi-level deck, and treehouse by the second week in June. We moved in our bedroom set within a day. Now we could have family over. The cottage was beautiful and cozy but did not lend itself to a lot of people being able to move, sit, or stand. The build in benches were great, because we didn't need furniture and had more space. I did, however, buy lots of outdoor pillows and cushions. We put an overabundance of flowers of different varieties in the build in planters. The centerpiece wall fountain was large with three tiers, a little over the top but, really cool.

Cole build an arch at the bottom of the steps of the deck into the yard. It wasn't as professional looking, but I planted Sweet Pea vines and used lots of Miracle Grow. I knew the nieces and nephews would love the tree house. We didn't have a pool but cooking smores and a tree house were just as cool as a pool.

The summer brought weekends filled with Cole's family barbeques, pool parties, mini vacations at his parents' beach house. We watched movies on bed sheets with our nieces and nephews and camped in our backyard. We went to adventure theme parks, camping, hiking, road trips to different states, with the nieces and nephews from both sides of the family and we all grew close knit that summer we would never forget and would continue to come together each summer. From my sadness, a new family grew, and the love and happiness knew no bounds.

The last Saturday of summer break I met with Margaret. You are so lucky to be retired, I have a few more years to go. Yea, Cole has 12 more years before he wants to retire. Lisa let's do lunch at La Casa; we haven't been there in a long time. Sure, Cole took the pups to his sister's house and won't be back until after 2:00 so I am hungry, yea I am always hungry. We drove over and the waitress took us to the back where the larger room was. SURPRISE! A baby shower really! I am very surprised. I thought you would be, Cole is actually watching the kids. The room was filled with teachers, friends, and family.

The gluten-free food was great, the cake icing was even better. Presents for baby were over the top. Margaret how do you manage to find the time for everything. Honey, I learned from you how to make lists. You have the runner stroller, a convertible crib, car seat and high chair that changes as the baby grows, wipes, and diapers galore for every stage. You have clothes for all the stages up to 24 months. A baby bath set with lotions, and toys for the tub. Cole made the toy chest, and everyone put in toys and books.

I told everyone you were too old to remember what to get. Thanks, I am old. Yea you are to most people who believe you are 45; remember we had your birthday party the day of the memorial, so most people think you are now 45 years old. Good point Margaret. Sometimes I forget there is too much to remember. That's why you have me. The baby shower took a long time as I personally kissed and hugged everyone that was there and let them know how grateful I was to have loving caring women in my life.

Cole and Mike came to help load up all the gifts and the toy chest he had made. Thank you, Mike, so much for the beautiful gift. Mike smiled, if I could just convince my wife a car would be a great birthday gift, and chance you could talk to her?

The close of the summer was sad. Cole would be going back to school; I would get to stay in bed and sleep in. Cole would be taking off six weeks of school when we had the baby. So, the first week back to school I helped Cole and Margaret get started and plan for when he would be home with me and the baby.

My hair and baby were growing fast. My hair was about 5 inches, so I had it styled short and put away the head scarf. Cole thought my hair cut made me look like a teenager. My baby bump was growing, and I looked like a pregnant teenager.

We had talked about how many people would be wondering when I got pregnant. We decided that friends are friends and no judgement is needed with true friends.

The OB-GYN had me coming in for visits every week now. Since this was this body's first baby, he said the baby would probably come late, and I should be prepared for a quick labor. What do you mean a quick labor? He said since I was still very active, in great health and didn't gain a lot of weight, I would probably deliver quickly. I had only gained 16 pounds, and my flowing dresses didn't reveal much. Since I had Nicole with only four hours of labor, he suggested that Cole and I become acquainted with giving birth in an emergency DVD.

PART 3

The fourth week of September I went for my visit with Gertrude. We were meeting now every other month. I am so glad you had a wonderful summer and are bonding with your new family, Gertrude said. I am and my life is full and so is my tummy. Baby will be coming any day in the next few weeks. I have finally let go of the past and dwelling on what

I had lost. I focus on all the riches I have now and that the past made me ready for the future.

Gertrude walked me to the door then asked, do you have names picked out for the baby. No, I told Cole that he would pick out the name when she was born. Oh, you are having a girl. Well, I feel like it's a girl. I hugged Gertrude which had now become our ritual and the warmth glowed on her face. Maybe a puppy for Gertrude I thought, I would have to call Greta and ask what she thought.

My routine didn't vary much as I stopped at WAWA to pick up a chilly dog and soda. Then off to see Dr. Light. I was seeing him every other month as well because it was getting to busy with the baby coming. I was in perfect health and so was the baby. I would be the first brain transplant to have a baby. There had been one other brain transplant since mine. The man was in eastern Europe and had become quite famous for about two months until he couldn't take all the attention and went into seclusion. He left his family so his children could finish school and didn't want to uproot them. For his wife it had to be odd having a different man's body for your husband and father. It would be hard for children to look at another man and call him dad. I didn't want anyone to know about me and now I could see how family would suffer.

Dr. Light was waiting for me at the door with an office chair in front of him. Sit! I laughed and sat down in the chair he wheeled me to the table. You will be having the baby any day now. Yes, I wish I could just be wheeled around everywhere. He took blood and checked all my vitals. You are doing wonderful. Your health is good, and your mental state is great. Not many people could go through what you have and be able to pull through on the, what's the term, bright side of things. Just bright side.

Well, at first I thought it was harder having my daughter's body and would have been easier having a stranger's body, but now, knowing someone has to die for this to happen, I am much happier in my daughter's body because I will always have her heart giving me a reason to live and giving me life just like the day she was born.

Dr. Light coughed and wiped his eyes. That was the most beautiful thought of a mother about her child I have ever heard. Now, my eyes were getting watery. Once you have a child you never see yourself again. Dr. Light walked over to his desk and opened his drawer to pull out a wrapped gift. This is for when baby is born. Thank you that is so kind and thoughtful.

When I got home; I put the gift in the baby's room still wrapped. Tonight, I was making dinner. Well, not really, my friend Allison baked lasagna and dropped it off at the house. I could make a great salad, and toast garlic bread like nobody's mother. Cole was impressed that my culinary skills had improved. He was still taking lessons and I joined him in class. I only had one month under my belt; he had over a year. I never knew that the way you cut and when you cut your food can make a difference in taste and nutrition.

After dinner clean up and praises about how wonderful the lasagna was, we walked the pups around the park path. The days were getting shorter now. I told Cole about my appointments and how Gertrude could use a puppy. Dr. Light gave the baby a gift, I left it in her room. Her! No, I don't know for sure I was just using that pronoun. Oh, I thought you had another ultra sound and found out. No, I do want it to be a surprise. I want you to know that for some reason I just feel like baby is a girl. So, Cole have you been thinking of names for her or him. I have, but I am not telling you until he or she is in your arms. Please don't use Norman or Egbert. No, I have reasonable names picked out. Ok, when the kid gets old enough, I am telling them it's your fault for everything; you named him or her.

Ouch, baby is moving around like push-ups. I stopped on the path and reached for his hand and placed it on the moving area of my baby bump.

Whoa, I feel an arm or leg moving that is so cool. Cool, really that's the word you use for a human being moving around inside me trying to get out. Sorry. No, Cole I was just kidding or just baby hormones. I have been having pains or Braxton Hicks false labor pains. Why didn't you say something? It's false labor and there was no need to worry you. I go to the doctor's weekly now and he told me that it could be soon like within a week. I am only slightly dilated. When I had Nicole, I had these false labor pains for 2 to 3 days then nothing and she was born almost two weeks later. Let's go back to the word dilated that means what, that the opening is widening for a baby to come through? Yes, and it is normal. We got this Cole. The Braxton Hicks prepare the body for birth, it's all normal.

Hand me Bella's lease you are officially no longer walking or running the pups any more. What! Remember I am the king and what I say goes. I started laughing so hard until another cramp took my breath away. I want you to tell me every time you feel something even if it's fake.

When we got home, we changed for bed, and all four of us cuddled together. Cole held the phone with the camera turned on as Max played peek-a-boo. In Max's little girl voice with her paws waving around while she talks, since I have Cole to hold the camera now, "What do dogs eat for breakfast?

Pooched eggs.". We both were amazed at how many thousands of hits these Max vids were getting, Nicole was right. Hey Lisa, don't forget we have our Grief Counseling Group tomorrow night. Yes, that means taco Tuesday. I will make cookies and cupcakes with vanilla frosting for group.

During the night I had to get up and pee. The false labor pains were hitting me every hour. I found that if I walk around rubbing baby it would calm down. Standing and swaying back and forth helped also. I nudged and pushed my way back into bed as the Max like to spread out. Bella was more polite and curled up in a ball to sleep. I whispered; Cole I am having false labor pains. I know, came the response that scared the bejeebers out of me. I didn't realize you were fully awake you scared me. I thought I would wake you gently I said in a whisper. Or you thought I wouldn't wake up and know but that you truthfully can say you told me. Cole, why do you have to be Wright! We both laughed and cuddled together. Are you sure you are ok? Yes, they went away, and no baby came so we are good.

The next morning, we did our routine, I made coffee and packed his lunch, Cole made eggs benedict. Can you have undying devotion for a man who makes the best hollandaise sauce? We kissed each other good bye, I took the pups for a slow walk around the park path and talk to the moms and kids at the park

• • •

while the pups jump into the little lake. I would on Tuesdays make cookies and cupcakes for group. Then, I get his clothes ready for the next day of school. After that I vacuum Max and what hair she has deposited. He picks up nacho cheese taco Supremes and we sit outside at the picnic table where people walk or jog by on the park path otherwise known as people watching.

While we were eating our tacos, Cole asked about my day. I have been having more false labor pains but as long as I keep moving around and keep my mind busy; I am fine. I went to the store and bought storage bins so I could reorganize all the Christmas ornaments. I explained to Cole, how every year Nicole would make a Christmas ornament and how I found the ornament in her back pack after the plane crash while I was still in the hospital. That sounds like a great family tradition, we should have baby start this year. That gives me an idea, we should have our nieces and nephews start next summer. Cole, I miss our nieces and nephews I had so much fun this summer I was actually sad they had to go back to school. Cole handed me the last taco; I know you want it. You know me pretty well. It's almost time to go.

On our way to group I asked Cole how long he has been going to group and how long for the others. Well, I have been going almost five years. Sam is the newest. Then you I suppose. Well, do you think they know when I make the cookies instead of you? I don't know Cole laughed. I mixed your cookies with some that I made. You are always surprising me. I grabbed Cole's hand so quickly it startled him. I pressed his hand on the moving body part in my belly. I feel it, he said with the biggest smile that made his face light up. So, do I. The cramps are coming more often like a few times each hour.

We went into group to find Sam with Lizzie. He was sitting next to Helen another group member, who was fussing over him and Lizzie. Oh, lookie there, Sam has a girlfriend, she came with him to the wedding. Maybe she just likes the puppy. Cole stop it. Look how happy they look together and both of them are smiling. During the meeting everyone had a chance to speak, then we got up for our social time and eating goodies. I nudged Cole, do you think she just likes the puppy.   We both laughed and I poked Cole, not so loud.

We drove home pondering the question of Sam's new girlfriend. We were joking and laughing the whole way home. We took the pups out for their nightly walk and then got ready for bed. The pups joined us, and Max wanted to do his peek-a-boo. Cole find a good joke for Max. He wrote down the joke and said, ok ready. I took Max's paws and did her peek-a-boo and in her little girlie voice I read the joke Cole had written down. "Why do dogs love conjunctions? They just love butts! I tried so hard not to laugh until we finished. I broke down laughing just imaging all the dogs at the dog park who sniff butts. I was laughing so hard my tummy hurt. I rolled over towards Cole who was laughing his silly laugh that meant he wasn't really laughing.

I got up to get something to drink and when I returned to bed Cole and the dogs were spread out so, I had no room. Alrighty then, you guys have to move over. COLE my water broke. I bent over and grabbed his arm. Cole jumped out of bed. Now, you mean now the baby is coming. I couldn't speak the pain hit me so hard that my face turned white. Cole pushed the dogs off the bed and helped me lay down. Bella and Max scurried out of the bedroom quickly. I feel like I have to push. You can't just have your water break and have the baby it takes hours. I need to push it's so strong. I will get your bag and the car keys. No, don't leave me I can feel the head, I can't get up. Call 911. A scream that shook the whole house made Cole drop the phone under the bed. I lifted my night gown and could feel the head. I felt like I would faint. COLE, now baby is here now!

Cole came up from under the bed with the phone in his hand. He looked at me and said who am I calling? Call 911. Within seconds I screamed again as he was trying to give our address. Cole you need to help me the head is coming out NOW! He looked and turned white and put the phone on speaker and told the responder that he could see the head. Cole did what the responder told him to do. I was so glad we had a poster bed. I never screamed so loud, not even in the movies. Our baby came within five minutes. He lay her on my chest. What is her name I asked still panting? Ariel is her name after the arch angel. Cole got up from the bed to let the responders in. They checked everything and asked Cole if he wanted to cut the cord. He did; but looked like he was going to faint. Cutting the cord was not as easy as it looks. The one responder told Cole to put elbow grease into it. When he finally cut the cord, relief washed over his face. I laughed softly as my throat was sore from screaming.

They took Ariel and I to the hospital. Cole drove behind the ambulance. He started the phone chain. His parents got there first, then Margaret, later our sisters and brothers. He was so happy to tell the story over and over again to everyone that came. His brother punched him in the shoulder saying, "Bro, I didn't know you had it in you. Me, I would have run." Everyone saw Ariel in the nursery. While everyone was admiring their new family member, Cole told the story again, from the beginning in case anyone hadn't heard the whole story yet. After everyone left Cole asked the nurse if he could hold Ariel. He told her the whole story too.

Cole came into my hospital room holding Ariel. She is so tiny and beautiful. Her eyes are looking at me. He kissed her softly on the head. I am so glad you delivered her and cut the cord; I am so proud of you. Cole looked at me and smirked, well now that I 've done that, never want to again. I don't know if I was more scared of your screaming or that we were having a baby. Well this will be a good story to tell our children and grandchildren won't it.

After a few hours of the three of us in the hospital bed together, the nurse came to break it up. I will go home and take care of the pups, and I guess clean up too. Oh, I forgot about that. I will come back later on today. He kissed me and Ariel good bye.

Margaret came by and snatched the Ariel right from me. This baby is so beautiful, yes Auntie Margaret is here for you sweetie pie. She looked at me and smiled. I would not have the energy for doing this all again. I am so glad Hannah and AJ are in college. We are middle aged. No, Margaret you are middle aged I am going to be 24 in another couple weeks. My mind tells me I am too old for this, but my body has lots of energy. I have already walked around the whole hospital 6 times. You know Lisa, I just realized as the years go by and we do our Saturday coffee date, you will always look younger than me. Yea, what a shame, but you are not older, just more mature looking than me. I want you to be her

Godmother. There is no one kinder or loving than you Margaret. She hugged me but wouldn't give me back my baby.

After Margaret left, I answered all my emails and texts and did a Facebook update on Max's new sister. Bella would need more of my time when I got home. I called Cole to ask him to bring me something for lunch. I would be able to check out tomorrow morning, but I was hungry. Cole answered the phone right away. Sorry I am not there yet; we have a little problem. What's wrong? Well the mattress is well, let's just say unusable and Mike helped me take it to the dump. We just left the mattress store, but delivery will won't be for three more days. So, we will be staying in the spare room in Nicole's bed. The pups are fine. I was just getting ready to come over. Great, could you pick up a pepperoni pizza? I will love you even more and for eternity and beyond.

We sat and enjoyed hot pizza. You know that nurse gave me a dirty look when she saw I was coming in with a pizza. Maybe we should save her a piece. Good luck with that you never leave any behind. I laughed a little too loud. Cole looked at me oddly. You know you have been laughing a lot lately. Maybe all the laughing is what made you go into labor. Yea, you're right, live, love, and laugh.

We brought Ariel home with family waiting for us. We all had lunch together then to my relief everyone left. I love his family and mine, but it was claustrophobic, and the pups were way too excited with the new baby.

Our new mattress hadn't come so went to lay down on Nicole's bed. Her bed was only a queen, so it was a tight squeeze. Of course, Bella and Max were there nudging for space. Did you order the extra-large king-size mattress? Yes, nothing else could fit us all. Our bedroom is truly a bed room. The bed fills up the whole room practically. After nursing Ariel, I lay her on Cole's chest to sleep.

I had to move around. I showered and took the pups for a short walk. I came home and wrote my thank you notes and read my emails. I emailed Cole's brother and asked him to build a bench swing for our yard. Cole's birthday was two days before Nicole's and was only a week away. I told him where I wanted it and asked if he could deliver it at night so Cole wouldn't see it until morning. I went on-line to the local garden shop and ordered five rose bushes. I wanted a red, pink, white, orange, and yellow. A different color for each I thought. One color each for Cole's wife, his daughter, my husband, Nicole, and Sam. This was perfect planting time. We wouldn't see any blooms until next year. Now, how to get Cole out of the house. He was now on family leave. I texted Margaret and told her my plans, she would know what to do.

I took my mirror and went outside with a cup of coffee, yep, de-cafe. Cole knew about my talking to the mirror coping strategy, but it felt weird with someone else around. I sat down and opened my compact and studied Nicole's face for a long time. You are a mama, and I know you are smiling and laughing at us. She is so tiny and happy. That's it! I did the smirk! I mastered the smirk of Nicole's, my favorite smirk I did it! I really did it perfect. I was smirking for so long I started to get self-conscious hoping nobody saw me smirking into a mirror in my back yard.

Mom you are a little nutty, but you make life so much fun. My baby is so beautiful just like you. Sam would have been such a proud daddy. I love that you are doing the rose bushes in memory of us. You are the best, funniest, smart, and beautiful mom and I know Ariel has the very second-best parents in the world. Your hair looks good too. Make sure Ariel gets hugs and kisses every single day, just like you did with me. Having that love everyday made me a better person. No, it made me a better person. **No, you made me a better person. I love you mom.** I love you too.

I went back into the house and let the pups out. Cole was in the living room rocking back and forth with Ariel in his arms. You're back, great she is sucking on my pinky, and I don't think she really likes it. Really, that was good thinking. I took Ariel and nursed her. Cole stood beside me watching her. When I talk, she looks at me, like now!

The following week we got Mike to get Cole out of the house the day before his birthday. His brother installed the bench swing into the back yard. Margaret helped me landscape and plant the five rose bushes around it. It actually looked professionally done. Girl high fives. This looks great like something out of a magazine. It does. After giving Cole a car for a wedding present do you think he is anticipating something more maybe. No, that's not Cole. Remember he has gone through a lot of changes. He moved into this house this year, so he has a new home, new wife, new baby in under a year. I would say you both have had a pretty overwhelming year.

I asked Cole if he wanted to go out to dinner for his birthday, and he said no, just wanted to play with the Ariel and the pups. Max is getting really attached to him. He calls her wolfie. He feels more manly with a wolf than a poodle.

His mom has the cake and his dad ordered food, so his family and my sister are coming over while I take him for a walk on the park path. They will come over with the food and decorations. When we get back everyone will be there. His mom is big on balloons like me. Or maybe she thinks he is still 5-years old, Margaret whispered. That could be I chuckled.

Margaret took my hand and said, it will be Nicole's birthday soon. Do you have any plans? I was going to visit her grave. Ok, I will come with you. It's dark now let's get inside and cleaned up before Cole comes back. That cute little baby should be awake by now, if not, I am waking her. Don't you dare.

Cole came home from Mike's about 10:30 and found us all in bed waiting for him. Our new mattress gave all of us room. Your subjects all happy you are home. He laughed and got into bed. So, I want to start running or a light jog tomorrow how does that sound. Ok, that stroller is really neat. Good night Mr. Wright. Good night Mrs. Wright.

I got up early and made coffee, eggs, and toast and served Cole breakfast in bed. Happy Birthday! Let's have our coffee outside. We all went outside and sat.

Ariel is such a good sleeper and slept through the night so far, keeping my fingers crossed. Cole took a sip of coffee and watched as the pups went to their potty area, then noticed the bench swing. Whoa, what is that. Happy Birthday!

He went over and sat on the swing, this looks like it's been here, and the plants, when on earth did you do this! Your brother made it and brought it over last night and Margaret helped me landscape. Are those rose bushes. Each one is a different color for our lost family members. I sat down next to him still nursing Ariel.

This is really special. Tears welled in his eyes. Cole, what is it? I am just so happy that I have been given another chance at life with a wonderful wife and baby. We swung in silence for a long time. I put Ariel in his arms and let him enjoy his new birthday present.

It was almost noon when the five of us started on the park path. Cole had wolfie and the stroller and I had Bella. Cole's head couldn't be any higher. I laughed and he just looked at me. You are a great man Cole, you love your wolfie and Ariel and it's your birthday. I am happy very happy man. After we finish our walk lets have lunch in the backyard and spend the day there. Sounds good to me. Wait till you see who will be in the back yard waiting for you I thought.

When we walked off the park path and into our back yard, Cole jumped. Surprise! I am too old for birthday parties. Nonsense, the surprise keeps you jumping. The afternoon was fun; and everyone was holding Ariel. I took lots of pictures for our new family photo album.

Two days later, I had Ariel in her baby wrap, and I stood in front of Nicole's head stone. Hey, my baby girl, we miss you so much. Cole and I talked it over and we think Ariel should know her mom and about her dad. Your friend Crystal gave me lots of photos and your letters from Sam. We aren't telling family, because that would be just too weird. We will tell Ariel that it's our family treasure secret. Having a baby at my brain's stage of life I know so much more. I know I couldn't stay at home when you were born, and I am so sorry that I wasn't able to. Ariel will make her first Christmas ornament and we will continue the tradition. Maybe one day Ariel will say the same thing I do, and say to me, "you say the same thing over and over".

Ariel gets a two for one deal. Cole loves Ariel so much and I can tell they will be close. This time around, he will be taking the pictures not me.

6 Years Later

Mommy the wrapping on the ornament is coming off. I turn around and say it's ok sweetie you are going to unwrap it anyway to hang on the tree. I hope mommy and grandma like it. I am sure they will, I do. We all got out of the car and Ariel and I walked hand in hand to Nicole's head stone. We had planted a tiny evergreen tree and each year we made two special ornaments, one for our tree and one for here.

Your mommy's thoughts are here and your grandma's body. Mommy, you mean my mommy's brain and my mommy's mom's body. As we reached the head stone Ariel put the ornament on a tiny branch. I turned around to see Cole standing far off. He was holding 5-year-old Michael's hand and carrying 3-year-old Emma close to him.

So, tell me again the family treasure secret Ariel asked. We were in an accident; Nicole's brain didn't work, and I didn't have body so the doctors put my brain in my daughter's body so she could still live. So, you look like my mommy. But who do I look like? YU.